Items should be returned to a library by closing time on or before the date stamped, unless a renewal has been granted

Constable Along the Trail

By the same author

The Constable Series

Constable on the Hill
Constable on the Prowl
Constable Around the Village
Constable Across the Moors
Constable in the Dale
Constable by the Sea
Constable Along the Lane
Constable Through the Meadow
Constable in Disguise
Constable Among the Heather
Constable by the Stream
Constable Around the Green
Constable Beneath the Trees
Constable in Control
Constable in the Shrubbery
Constable Versus Greengrass
Constable About the Parish
Constable at the Gate
Constable at the Dam
Constable Over the Stile
Constable Under the Gooseberry Bush
Constable in the Farmyard
Constable Around the Houses
Constable Along the Highway
Constable Over the Bridge
Constable Goes to Market
Constable Along the River-bank
Constable in the Wilderness
Constable Around the Park

CONSTABLE AT THE DOUBLE
Comprising
Constable Around the Village
Constable Across the Moors

HEARTBEAT OMNIBUS
Comprising
Constable on the Hill
Constable on the Prowl
Constable in the Dale

HEARTBEAT OMNIBUS VOLUME II
Comprising
Constable Along the Lane
Constable Through the Meadow

NICHOLAS RHEA

Constable Along the Trail

ROBERT HALE · LONDON

First published in Great Britain 2005

ISBN 0 7090 7755 6

Robert Hale Limited
Clerkenwell House
Clerkenwell Green
London EC1R 0HT

A catalogue record for this book is available from the British Library

2 4 6 8 10 9 7 5 3 1

Typeset in 12/15pt Baskerville by
Derek Doyle & Associates, Liverpool.
Printed in Great Britain by
St Edmundsbury Press Limited, Bury St Edmunds, Suffolk.
Bound by Woolnough Bookbinding Limited.

Chapter 1

After World War II, the motor car was increasingly used as a source of pleasure for the ordinary family and one development from this was the motor rally, later being known as the treasure hunt. I think the term 'motor rally' had become rather confusing and slightly alarming because it echoed the highly professional nationwide RAC Rally and other high-speed and high profile contests approaching that status. In those cases, high powered cars complete with their navigators, entourage of mechanics, spare parts vehicles, travelling workshops and supporters, hurtled through forests, country parks and even along public roads in a competitive manner, whereas ordinary people simply wanted a pleasureable means of seeing parts of the countryside they might not otherwise visit. Family orientated low-key treasure hunts provided that kind of gentle and interesting outing for groups of families and friends, even if they were tinged with a slight competitive edge. Staff in offices and factories also organized this kind of outing as a social get-together.

Those motorized treasure hunts were ideal for those who did not wish to indulge in fierce, split-second competitions against semi-professionals aided by back-up teams. Instead, they offered the chance to potter along the lanes and enjoy the countryside with some entertainment and interesting information along the way, then finish at a pleasant inn with a snack and a few drinks as the participants discussed their experiences.

These modest so-called mini-rallies or treasure hunts revealed parts of the countryside and provided facts about it in a very pleasant way, although they varied considerably in the way they were organized and run. They ranged from the highly efficient to the grossly inefficient, while catering for trips by the whole family or just part of it, or for the staff of offices and factories, clubs and societies. There is no doubt they became very popular but the adverse effect was that some pretty villages were swamped with one or more groups of excited motorists every summer evening or Sunday afternoon. The peace and tranquillity was shattered. Some of the organizers – and indeed some of the participants – were not the most efficient neither were they the most considerate of people. Many were downright selfish and rude. Drivers got lost, they went miles off route so that they had to break speed limits to successfully complete the competition, they drove into private properties, they dropped litter, they swore at villagers and committed an almost endless list of nuisances, not to mention the inevitable range of road traffic offences. It did not take long for the authorities to decide this new and growing form of motorized fun should be subjected to some form of control.

Races and trials of speed between motor vehicles was already illegal on public highways but these amateur treasure hunts/rallies were not considered to be either races or trials of speed. Indeed, the best were organized so that penalty points were incurred by any competitor who exceeded a speed limit or committed any road traffic offence.

The events were usually planned around a specific route which involved some basic map-reading, careful time-keeping without breaking speed limits and the noting of sights along the way. Those sights had to be entered on the competitor's route sheet as proof of that car's adherence to the specified route – such things might be the date on the front of a certain building, the name of a house on a road junction or the name of the patron saint of a village church. Almost anything in fact.

Such a clue might even be the name of the landlord of the Kings Head, the species of tree or flower growing in a particular location or the identification of an object standing on the village green. An accurate noting down of these facts was vital to the competition. Points were awarded for each correct answer and in some cases, competitors had to record the time they passed check points, or there might even be a marshal to sign their sheets with a note of the time, these being useful means of controlling their speed and recording their presence at a correct place en route.

For the villagers whose homes became targets, there was little enjoyment. Imagine pensioners sitting quietly with a glass of wine in their front garden on a warm and sunny Sunday afternoon only to be confronted by hordes of motorists stopping outside to peer over the hedge to obtain the date carved above the front door of their cottage. Or think of the landlord of the Kings Head being asked his name by scores of people rushing into his bar but not buying anything when in fact his name was prominently printed above his main entrance, or think perhaps of the landlord of the Crown who was asked by treasure hunters for a take-away sample of his triangular shaped beermats.

There were hundreds of such incidents, many of which involved rudeness or perhaps mere thoughtlessness by both the organizers and the competitors.

In the 1960s, this kind of event was controlled by section 36 of the Road Traffic Act of 1962. It said, 'A person who promotes or takes part in a competition or trial (other than a race or trial of speed) involving the use of motor vehicles on a public highway commits an offence unless the competition or trial is authorized and is conducted in accordance with any conditions imposed by or under Regulations.'

Later the Motor Vehicles (Competitions and Trials) Regulations of 1969 were enacted to regulate the holding of competitions or trials (other than races or trials of speed) involving the use of motor vehicles on a public highway. This meant that the organizers had to plan the event with sufficient advance notice to get it approved by the local chief constable. He required details of the proposed event, with dates and times, a copy of the route, a note of the average speed (which was usually rather low, say, 20 m.p.h. and any other relevant factors, such as the presence of marshals or check points, any permission to drive through specified private properties like forests or country estates and the arrangements for a safe and secure place to finish, usually off the road. If he was satisfied with all the arrangements, the chief constable would authorize the treasure hunt, perhaps incorporating further conditions such as: villagers along the route should be notified in advance; no participating vehicle should be unroadworthy; the event should end by no later than 9.30 p.m.; there should be an interval of at least one minute between each competitor's start; that no infants or animals be carried, no litter deposited and no undue noise or disturbance caused.

The chief constable would not authorize such a hunt if one was already scheduled to take place at the same time in the same area and so a positive but acceptable form of control began to make these hunts more tolerable to country dwellers.

Due to its charm and location, it was not surprising that Aidensfield was a popular venue for treasure hunts. Some events passed through en route to different places while others terminated at the local pub for the inevitable inquest over a few drinks and a bar snack. As a result of the controls instituted by the 1962 Road Traffic Act, I was always notified by Force Headquarters of any treasure hunt scheduled to enter any of the villages on my patch. As a consequence, I made sure that those in charge of places like the pub, school, church, post office, shop and elsewhere were aware of its date, time and route. Not every authorization contained a provision that those living along the route should be personally informed but the villagers themselves generally managed to spread word to those who might be affected. It was known, for example, that almost every such hunt included the questions – 'What is the number of Aidensfield Railway Bridge?', 'What is the first name on Aidensfield War Memorial?' and 'What is the date above the door of the Aidensfield cottage with the crooked chimney?' Another was 'What is the name of the large house behind the gates bearing two eagles?'

And so it was that I received advance notification that the Ashfordly and District Corkscrew Collectors Club (ADCCC) was about to stage a treasure hunt in the general vicinity of Aidensfield.

It would finish at the pub where competitors and organizers would have a snack as they argued and discussed their impressions of the rally. It was to be held on the last Friday in June with some thirty cars participating and one of the features was to be a display in the pub of some remarkable, historic and valuable corkscrews. It was expected they would provide added interest to the evening.

The inn's hosts, ex-Sergeant Oscar Blaketon and Gina Ward were very happy to cater for the gathering and agreed to put on a welcome-home meal which included pork pies, sausage rolls, ham sandwiches, chicken portions, home-made fruit cake, cheese and biscuits.

'It's a regular event, they've been here before, Nick,' Oscar Blaketon reminded me when I was chatting to him about the treasure hunt. 'They'll be no trouble.'

'It seems quite a well-organized event,' I said.

'It is, and they're a friendly bunch of coves, completely hooked on corkscrews, that's all they talk about but they stage this treasure hunt every year as a social event for family and friends, a sort of thank-you for tolerating their non-stop corkscrew talk over the preceding months. They don't finish up here every time, though, I reckon it's about five years since they were last in here, before I retired from the job, that was. But I'm assured it's always a good evening, they're a sociable lot and very good spenders!'

I established that the first competitor to arrive at the finish in the paddock behind the pub was expected around eight thirty that Friday evening, with the others theoretically coming home at one minute intervals.

That assumption was based on the hope they did not get lost, didn't suffer a puncture or breakdown or didn't get involved in some other mishap. I anticipated no problems with car parking or the extra crowds the event would generate, nor did I expect any troublesome behaviour from them. Having finished my day's duty, I was free that evening but didn't think it necessary to ask one of the Ashfordly constables to supervise the hunt's return in my absence. Because it was my evening off, Mary and I thought we would pop into the pub to enjoy the atmosphere and perhaps learn something about corkscrews.

We arrived shortly before eight thirty to find the paddock behind the pub had been well equipped and signed as the finishing point; well-placed off the road, it would also double as the competitors' car park. Standing near the gate was a marshal wearing a bright red cap, red sweater and white trousers very identifiable and highly visible. He was carrying a clipboard and above him was a banner stretched between two poles; it bore the letters 'ADCCC' and the word 'Finish', also in red. A small crowd of eager spectators stood around awaiting the return of the first competitor but Mary and I did not join them. We did not know any of these people and so we went into the pub, ordered our drinks and found a vacant table which we claimed before the anticipated crowds came in from the finishing line.

'They all set off from Ashfordly town centre car park,' Blaketon explained as I was buying our drinks. 'You'll have seen a copy of the route? And the questions? That was all top secret before the event, of course, not to be seen by the competitors.'

'Yes, thanks, I got a copy.'

'Well, with an average speed of only twenty miles an hour, I can't see anyone is likely to get over-heated! There are plenty of clues so they shouldn't get lost, but they've got to work out the route from clues. It's not too easy, in fact it's quite a challenge, I'd say.'

'It's a tough set of questions but they're used to that sort of thing and it gives them a nice run around the moors while taking in some splendid scenery. So who's this chap Smithers named on the sheet?'

'He's the organizer, he's last year's winner,' he smiled. 'That's how they do it. Whoever wins this year's run will have to organize next year's and so on. The snag is that not all the winners are very capable organizers but from what I've seen of it so far tonight, it seems fairly well run with plenty of marshals around the course. You can't miss 'em, they're all dressed in red and they all came here to see the finishing line before heading off to their points, so they're all familiar with the entire route. That's how they do things in the modern world of corkscrew enthusiasts. Very efficiently, I'd say.'

I returned to Mary but as time passed while we enjoyed our drinks, I gradually became aware of some anxiety among the treasure hunt's organizers and marshals. One of the marshals came into the bar to ask Blaketon if he'd received telephone calls from any of the competitors or marshals out on the moors, the latter being rather unlikely as they were usually positioned in remote places with no convenient telephone. But none of the competitors had rung in either. It seemed none was in distress.

Blaketon confirmed he'd had no such calls and I saw them all glance at their watches and at the bar clock. It was nearly nine o'clock and it was clear that not one of the competitors had returned; the first had been expected at half past eight but in spite of that, there was no other indication of a problem. Even so, I began to wonder if there was cause for concern.

When I went to refill our glasses, I mentioned that none had returned so far and expressed my view that they seemed to be running late. Blaketon said, 'There could be a problem, Nick. The first should have been back half an hour ago. In fact, they should have all been back by now, so I hope nothing's gone haywire.'

'You can always expect some delays in events of this kind,' I spoke from experience, having both organized and taken part in such treasure hunts. 'Timings are never very accurate and things like diversions or road works can seriously alter things.'

'I appreciate that, but our friend Smithers told me he'd checked the route umpteen times, the last occasion being tonight about an hour before the hunt started.'

'Is he here?' I asked.

'Yes, he's outside, waiting at the finish. He's more than a bit worried, I can tell you. They are very late, Nick, all of them, all long overdue. Smithers is the one with the red straw hat, by the way, it sets him apart from the others. He's going round asking if anyone's heard anything. You might want to talk to him, although it's not really your problem. Not yet, anyway!'

I wondered if Blaketon was still thinking like a police sergeant. 'You don't think there's any need for me to get involved?' I asked, momentarily reverting to my former role as his subordinate.

'I can't see why you should,' he said. 'You're off duty and it's not a police matter; it's by no means a major disaster. It seems to me they've simply got lost, all of them, strayed off the route for some reason which suggests they'll all realize it any time now and find their way back here. If only one was missing for a long time, then we might have reason to be worried, but if they're all missing, the chances are they'll all be together somewhere. If there's a real problem, they're bound to ring in soon, you can't just lose thirty cars and their passengers, even in the wide open spaces of our moors. My guess is they'll think their extra route and time is all part of the treasure hunt, whatever's happened to them.'

As the minutes ticked by with no sign of any treasure hunters and no messages, Mr Smithers and his colleagues began to grow highly concerned. They huddled in little groups and chattered, checking their watches as they repeatedly asked Blaketon if there'd been any telephone calls and when he said there hadn't, they all went back to the finishing line to wait and wait. There was so little they could do because they could be anywhere on those moors. Where could one begin to make a search? Half past nine arrived with no competitors returning. At that point, Mr Smithers came into the bar to seek further advice from Blaketon, no doubt recalling his previous service as a police sergeant.

'Mr Blaketon, this is very worrying, they're all overdue. Do you think someone should go and look for them?'

'You had thirty cars at the starting point, Mr Smithers, that's at least sixty people, probably more,' Blaketon reminded him with the people in the bar listening to this conversation, including me, and so I moved closer in case I was needed. 'It's most unlikely they've all got lost, or all been involved in accidents at the very same time, or all been taken ill or whatever. They know where the finishing line is, it's right here; that was given on their instructions and so they could call us if there's a problem. I've had no calls, the phone is in full working order and we've been on the premises all evening. No one's called, Mr Smithers, which suggests to me that your competitors don't recognize there is a problem even if you think there is. And if just one of your cars has had problems, it wouldn't take all the other twenty-nine to provide assistance. Because something is affecting all of them, I reckon they've mis-read the route, Mr Smithers. I think they've all gone steaming down the wrong road somewhere, but if you are really worried, then PC Rhea, over there, would be happy to notify his Control Room so that a search can be made. I'd say a pile-up involving thirty cars wouldn't be too difficult to trace!'

'I can ring Control anyway,' I offered. 'I can check whether they've had any unusual reports involving thirty cars. If I do that, it should eliminate some of your concern.'

'Use my phone,' offered Blaketon.

I rang the Force Control Room and spoke to PC Blenkin.

After I'd explained the problem over some good humoured banter, PC Blenkin assured me there had been no reports of a multiple road traffic accident, no reports of a motorcade being lost or being sighted in strange places, no reports of dozens of people with dazed expressions milling about in villages and no complaints from villagers about any mass invasion of their privacy. He did say, however, that he would alert his colleagues to the possibility that thirty cars were lost on the moors and would ring the pub if he received any information of value to us.

I returned to join Mary who was in danger of being ignored as I was gradually drawn into this dilemma but Blaketon followed me with a copy of the route in his hands, along with the questions and map references which were supposed to guide the competitors. Mr Smithers was with him. He was a tall, smart gentleman in his fifties with a balding head, dark horn rimmed spectacles and a neat little moustache. They pulled up chairs and settled at our table.

'This is PC Rhea, the local constable,' Blaketon introduced me. 'He knows every inch of these moors, Mr Smithers. This is his wife, Mary. Nick and Mary, this is Reg Smithers, the organizer. We've had another chat and we think the only answer is they've all mis-read the route directions and finished up in the wrong place.'

'That seems the most logical answer,' I agreed.

'Mr Smithers has suggested he goes right around the route himself, following his own instructions to see where they might have gone astray.'

'That won't help, will it?' I said. 'If Mr Smithers follows his own set of directions, he won't get lost like them, will he? And if they've diverted from the correct route, he'll not find them, will he? All he can do is follow his own route, he'll have no idea where they left it.'

'Ah,' said Smithers. 'No, of course not.'

'I think an independent person should check the route,' was my suggestion. Fortunately, it was Mary who offered the first glimpse of light by saying, 'Nick, these instructions don't actually say the hunt finishes at this pub, do they?' She had a copy which had been placed on each of the tables for the benefit of those who'd come to the finish, like us.

'Yes, it does,' nodded Smithers. 'The competitors follow the instructions which take them around the route and at the end it says 'Finish at the sign of the dancing blue dragons. They know it will be a pub, we always finish at a pub.'

'That's our pub sign,' agreed Blaketon. 'The coat of arms under the name of the pub shows a pair of blue dragons, standing on their hind legs.'

'Yes, but it doesn't say it is *this* pub,' Mary stressed.

'You're saying there are other inn signs with blue dragons?' I asked, suddenly realizing she was right.

'Well, yes, any of those belonging to Ashfordly Estate, or which used to belong to the estate. It's Lord Ashfordly's coat of arms, isn't it?'

'And the estate used to own more than a dozen pubs hereabouts, before they were sold off,' said Blaketon who was now studying the wording of the instructions.

I added, 'If they've all kept their original inn signs since being sold, Mary could be right, Mr Smithers. You don't specifically state the finish is here in Aidensfield.'

'No, but it's pretty obvious, isn't it? If you follow the directions. We used the Ordnance Survey map for this area as well, the instructions said all competitors must have an up-to-date edition, and we used only those roads on it which are coloured red, brown or yellow. That rules out unmetalled road, private roads and drives, green lanes and minor unfenced roads. We always do that, in all our hunts.'

'It would seem to me that the route is not as obvious as you had hoped, Mr Smithers,' said Blaketon. 'I suggest we all go into the snug, where it's quiet, and follow your directions as if we're on that treasure hunt. Nick knows these roads like the back of his hand, and I've a good working knowledge of them as well. It seems to me, Mr Smithers, that they've all mis-interpreted your instructions and finished up at the wrong pub.'

'But there'll be no marshals there to receive them, no finishing line, no one to tot up their points, no display of corkscrews, none of the things they'd expect.'

Mary chipped in again. 'It says there will be a surprise for them at the finish.'

'That's the display of historic and antique corkscrews,'

stressed Smithers. 'They belong to the uncle of one of our members, he offered to lend it for display tonight, that's the surprise.'

'A nice touch, Mr Smithers,' I laughed. 'But if all your treasure hunters have gone to the wrong pub, they will not know it's the wrong place, will they? They'll think they've all done the right thing and that it's the organizers who've got lost!'

'Or they might suspect the surprise is something to do with the fact no one's there to meet them!' chuckled Mary. 'They'll all be waiting there, waiting for something surprising to happen!'

'There's many a true word spoken in jest,' grinned Blaketon. 'Come along, into my snug and I'll get us all another drink apiece, on the house, as we try to get this thing sorted. Gina can look after the bar for the time being.'

With a map spread across a large table and with each of us supplied with a set of directions along with the answers to the clues, Blaketon, Mary, Smithers and I set about trying to fathom the destination of the missing hunters.

'We started from the town centre car park in Ashfordly,' said Smithers. 'And the first clue is 'Bank to the right as you head east.'

'That's obvious,' I agreed. 'Barclays Bank is on the corner as you leave the car park, and the road heads east . . .'

'Right,' and so I began to follow the route on the map. With Smithers in possession of the answers to his clues, it did not take long to follow the route and we used a domino as a car, moving it along the roads on the map as we mentally traced the route. Things went extremely well. We found our way around the route until we were only a short distance from the finish, having executed a circular path through some of the most beautiful parts of the moors. Then, quite literally on the final stretch with about three miles to go, we came to a remote junction high on the moors; from our approach it was Y-shaped. We were heading along the leg of the Y and had the choice of following either of the arms.

The clue said, 'Sounds like you – go along here.'

I looked at the map and spotted Yew Grange about a mile along the route. Yew sounds like 'you', I realized and so I said, 'We take the right hand fork.'

'No,' said Smithers. 'You should take the left. Yew Tree Farm is along there, just a few hundred yards to the left. Much closer than Yew Grange anyway.'

'You can't go that way,' I said. 'The road to the left is shown as white . . . I went along there only this afternoon, to Yew Tree Farm. There's a short stretch of unmade road just before you get to the farm. It's only about half a mile long but definitely shown as white on this map.' And I prodded it with my finger. 'And the instructions say that only roads shown in red, brown and yellow on this map are to be used.'

His face blanched. 'Oh no, I don't believe it . . .'

At this, each of us bent close to the map but the short stretch of white road was very clear to see. I knew how the competitors would have reacted upon arriving at that point – they'd have approached this junction, recognized the clue to Yew Tree Farm but then spotted the white road. Knowing they should not use white roads, they'd have regarded it as a clever trap . . . and the sight of Yew Grange along the alternative road, even at a considerable distance, would have assured them they were heading along the correct road. I would have done that and I knew from the expression of Mr Smithers' face, that he had made a very serious error.

'My fault . . .' he was most embarrassed. 'I checked it several times but didn't notice that bit of unsurfaced road . . . or didn't appreciate its importance. This is dreadful, I feel so stupid . . . but we've got to find them. Where can they have gone?'

There was only one more clue before the finish and when we read it, it was fairly innocuous. 'Bridge the beck and seek the blue dragons.'

Unfortunately, there was a bridge across a beck upon both of those routes and I could now see why the competitors had not recognized the error, but if one route led here, to the pub in Aidensfield, where did the other go?

'Ashfordly Hall,' said Mary as if reading my thoughts. 'It's got a big sign outside, hasn't it? With the blue dragons on it. The same coat of arms as the one on his pub. And it's along that road,' she was pointing to the map.

'Oh my God!' groaned Smithers. 'You mean all our people have gone to Ashfordly Hall? So why haven't they realized it was a mistake . . . I mean, you can't just drive into Ashfordly Hall and stay there, somebody would soon kick up a fuss. I'm sure Lord Ashfordly doesn't like his summer evenings interrupted by hordes of lost motorists!'

'The roads through the grounds are white on this map,' I laughed. 'That should have alerted them!'

'But there is a car park in a field at the side of the road, a yellow road,' Blaketon pointed out. 'It was often used in my day as the sergeant in Ashfordly, for the annual agricultural show, for example, or the sheep dog trials and lots of other events.'

'Fair enough,' I acknowledged. 'But if they all managed to get themselves to Ashfordly Hall, to park in that field, surely they'd realize something was wrong if Mr Smithers' officials weren't there to check them in?'

'Unless there was something else going on at the Hall?' smiled Mary in her gentle way.

'I'll ring them,' said Blaketon. 'I'll get through to the Estate office.'

From the phone at the end of the bar, he rang one of several numbers which served Ashfordly Hall, then said, 'Ah, Stan. Blaketon here in Aidensfield. Yes, I'm fine thanks. Now, I wonder if you can help me.'

He explained the problem, ending with 'Well, we've lost thirty cars and their passengers and we think they might have found their way into your grounds . . . is there something happening at the Hall tonight?'

Clearly, something *was* happening because Blaketon kept saying, 'Right, yes, I see, that could explain it . . . thanks, Stan.' And he replaced the phone to smile at us.

'There's a food and drink fair,' he told us. 'It's been going on all day since ten this morning – this morning it was trade only and this evening it's open to the public with exhibitions, a brass band, dancing in a marquee, drinks and so on. Quite a party, so Stan says, a good crowd has turned up. I remember something about it now, we got an invitation way back but couldn't go because we'd committed ourselves to catering for this treasure hunt.'

I knew nothing about it but Mary thought she'd seen a notice in the Gazette a week earlier, although I knew Ashfordly police would be aware of the event, if only from the point of view of increased traffic on the roads into town. But it was a low key event from a policing aspect, hence my non-involvement.

'So there would be a surprise for your competitors if they turned up at Ashfordly Hall?' I put to Mr Smithers. 'But you'd think they would realize the hunt didn't finish there, there'd be none of your marshals in attendance.'

'But they would find themselves among a lot of food, drink and happy people,' Mary laughed. 'I'm not surprised they stayed there, it sounds like a jolly sort of party to me!'

'I'd better go and find out,' said Smithers. 'I'll tell our marshal at your finishing line in the car park just in case any of them do turn up here . . .'

And so Mr Smithers jumped into his car and drove away to Ashfordly Hall, the time now being just after ten. Due to the lateness of the hour, the rest of us decided to remain here. After all, Blaketon and Gina had agreed to supply food and so those of us who had come to witness the prize giving settled down to enjoy the rest of the evening. Being the local bobby, however, I always felt it diplomatic to leave licensed premises at closing time and so, as there was no extension of hours, Mary and I made our farewells at ten thirty and went home. The supper, I should add, was very good indeed.

'I felt sorry for Mr Smithers,' Mary said as we walked along the main street. 'He'd obviously made a big mistake, well, a big one for that kind of outing.'

'As they all went to the wrong finish, I suppose they'll declare the contest null and void,' I said. 'No doubt we'll be told all about it in due course.'

It would be a couple of days later when I called at the pub, this time in uniform and on duty.

I was visiting all public houses on my patch to warn landlords about a load of whisky that had been stolen from a lorry on the A1; in such cases, there was always a likelihood the thieves would try to dispose of their haul through pubs and restaurants, offering the liquor at huge discounts.

'That curious business of the treasure hunt,' Blaketon said in his kitchen as he invited me in for a coffee. 'We were right, every competitor had gone to Ashfordly Hall. Luckily, the first one home was a previous organizer who knew the routine and straight away he realized none of the officials were there so he took over and checked everyone else in and got someone to add up the marks on their entry forms. The Ashfordly Hall staff were brilliant, guiding the cars into a separate area and so the corkscrew fans got a result. Because every one of the competitors had followed the directions and completed the same route, they accepted the result as genuine. It was a good decision, I thought. And so the winner could get the prize. The only thing they did not see was the collection of corkscrews, that had to be returned that night. I was glad to see them go, they were worth a fortune! But they all missed our supper!'

'So what happened to the unfortunate Mr Smithers?'

'It was a food and drink fair, and someone found a stall selling kitchen implements, so the treasure hunt competitors clubbed together and bought him a wooden spoon. They presented it to him before they left Ashfordly Hall – in fact, Lord Ashfordly did the honours even if he had no idea what it was all about.'

'So all's well that ends well, as they say?' I smiled.

'And I suppose I should add that famous quote which says, "For when the One Great Scorer comes, to write against your name, he marks – not that you won or lost but how you played the game." ' said Blaketon. 'I think they all played very well indeed.'

*

By following the trail provided by Mr Smithers on that occasion, we were able to come to a satisfactory conclusion, but another form of trail presented a problem to a group of runners known as the Ashfordly Harriers. Every year they held a paper-chase, then a popular means of having a bit of fun, a lot of exercise and raising money for the club. The winner received the Ashfordly Harriers Paper-Chase Cup which had been donated by the town's cricket club.

The paper-chase was always held in the summer at different locations in a variety of villages around Ashfordly, but it was inevitable that on occasions it returned to a former venue. It came to Aidensfield once every few years but when it did, the event was extremely popular with the runners because the rugged landscape offered the most demanding and varied of courses. There was lofty moorland, dense woodland and a track beside the river, as well as open fields and roads full of steep hills with lots of twists and turns. And with a gap of five years or so, it meant there were new runners on most occasions, therefore a change of route was not all that important.

The paper-chase, which covered a fairly gruelling course of ten miles, started and finished at the village cricket field when it came to Aidensfield.

The pavilion was utilized as tea rooms with the usual drinks and food. As it was a fund-raising event, spectators were charged to enter the cricket field, there was a raffle with good prizes and visitors were also expected to pay for their teas. Almost without exception, it was held on a Saturday in July, the date being a day when the village cricket team was not playing at home.

To keep the spectators interested and occupied while the runners were in action somewhere out of sight, there were stalls and various entertainments for adults and children alike. With up to a hundred runners taking part, having come from all over the district from a variety of athletic clubs, paper-chase day was one of the popular highlights of the Aidensfield summer season. For those unfamiliar with the sport, a paper-chase was really nothing more than a cross-country race but it was for runners on foot, not horse riders, cyclists or motor cyclists. It differed from a normal cross-country race in that the route was generally not known to the competitors before they started, and in the case of Ashfordly Harriers, it varied upon each return visit, if only slightly on some occasions. It was marked on the day, an hour or so before the scheduled start, by one or more non-racing runners tracing the route by dropping handsful of white paper which had been torn into small pieces. In most cases, the route markers carried large satchels full of the paper pieces which they sprinkled at key points; clearly, it was risky doing this on a very windy day and so the general practice was to mark the route very shortly before the race started while trusting the wind did not play havoc with the arrangements.

One factor, of course, was that each route marker was limited by the amount of paper pieces he could carry and so, on a long race, several of them would be deployed, dropping their bits of paper while starting at different points along the route. I am not sure from where they obtained the paper but I believe old newspapers provided most of the material; when scattered, it was rather like large pieces of white confetti, albeit sometimes with black print or photographs upon it. However, I never knew a competitor who had time to halt for a quiet read en route!

As I was not stationed at Aidensfield on the previous occasion the paper-chase had been held there, I had no experience of the event so when I received advance details, I found myself keen to go along and watch it. I knew there would be a good turn-out at the cricket field and made a diary entry of the date and time so that I could attend either on duty or off. Either way, I would make an effort to attend – but in spite of my youthful efforts at cross-country running, I had no intention of competing in the race! That was for youngsters much fitter than I.

But then, about three weeks before the great day, I received a visit from a man who had recently come to live in Aidensfield. His name was Ernest Ashcroft and he was a retired chemist; he and his wife had previously lived in Pontefract in the West Riding of Yorkshire and had retired to Aidensfield for a spot of peace and quiet. At ten o'clock one morning and accompanied by a small dog on a lead, Mr Ashcroft arrived at the office attached to my house. I was on duty, working on some reports which I was preparing to take to Ashfordly for the sergeant's attention and when I answered the doorbell, I saw a tall, smartly dressed gentleman in his mid-sixties.

He wore a trilby hat, a smart greenish sports jacket and matching trousers, a neat collar and tie and highly polished brown shoes. As a relative newcomer, I did not know him until that moment.

'Ah, Constable, I'm glad I caught you at home,' he smiled a thin smile as I stepped back to invite him into my modest place of work.

'Good morning, sir, how can I help?'

'You are PC Rhea?'

'I am, yes.' By now, he was inside the office and we stood at the counter as his little dog sniffed its way around the office as far as its lead would permit.

'Ernest Ashcroft,' he gave his name. 'I've just moved into Maple Tree Cottage on the main street. Retired from Pontefract, my wife and I. We fancied the country life, peaceful and quiet, as you can image after a hectic life-time in the chemical industry.'

'I know the cottage and Aidensfield *is* a nice quiet place, Mr Ashcroft.' I tried to sound happy for him. 'So how can I help you?'

'It's about that paper-chase that's coming to the village in a week or two's time, the Ashfordly Harriers event.'

'I've been told about it, everyone's looking forward to it.'

'It is illegal, you know. I thought I ought to point that out, just in case no one in authority has realized.'

'Illegal?' I was surprised at this comment. 'How is it illegal, Mr Ashcroft?'

'As a consequence of the Litter Act of 1958,' he said. 'Dropping litter in the countryside is illegal, as I am sure you know, just as throwing confetti outside churches is, so I thought I had better point that out before arrangements for the race get underway.'

'I'd never thought about it in that way,' I had to admit.

'Well, you can check on the law, Mr Rhea, and you will find I am right. I thought you might like to warn the organizers.'

'I'd be surprised if they weren't already aware of this.'

'I should hope so, but you can warn them I shall not hestitate to seek a prosecution if any offences are committed on that occasion. I dislike litter, you see, always have, Mr Rhea, and always will.'

'Yes, well, I'm sure you're right. I'll contact my sergeant at Ashfordly today, I shall be driving there very shortly, and I'll explain this to him. I know he'll deal with it immediately. Thank you for drawing our attention to this.'

'It is better to prevent such offences before they happen, I believe,' he said with his thin smile. 'Crime prevention in action, eh?'

'Absolutely, Mr Ashcroft.'

'Come along, Gipsy,' he said to his dog and they left in triumph to continue their walk.

I was aware that precise interpretation of the Litter Act, well meaning though it was, had caused problems because it wasn't as simple as Mr Ashcroft seemed to imply.

There was much more to it than merely dropping litter in the countryside – a good example would be an agricultural show in a village field. During the event, it could be guaranteed that a huge amount of litter would be dropped and abandoned but that kind of action never resulted in a prosecution. Conversely, if happy guests threw confetti over a bride and groom outside a church, they could risk prosecution. So what was the difference?

The answer lay in the wording of the statute which said, 'If any person without proper authority throws down, drops or otherwise deposits in, into or from any place *in the open air to which the public are entitled or permitted to have access without payment*, and leaves anything whatsoever in such circumstances as to cause, contribute to, or tend to lead to, the defacement by litter of any place in the open air, he shall be guilty of an offence.' The italics are mine. The Act went on to say that any covered place, open to the air on at least one side and available for public use, shall be treated as being a place in the open air.

A good example of the latter would be a bus shelter, so someone passing along the street who tossed a discarded fish-and-chip paper into a bus shelter would be guilty. Similarly, if someone walking along a street tossed a fish-and-chip paper into someone's private garden, they also committed an offence. The litter in the latter case was tossed from a place to which the public have access without payment, i.e. the street, but it defaced a private place in the open air, i.e. someone's garden. One important essence of the offence was that the litter must be left behind.

When the Act first came into force police officers would ask the litter lout to pick up his junk and place it in a bin – if he did so, then no offence was committed. Today, people who throw and abandon litter from motor vehicles while driving along our roads are clearly offending, as are those who leave their rubbish behind at picnic sites. Some of course, are no longer content with dropping cigarette packets or sweet papers – now they journey into the countryside to dump large waste household items such as refrigerators, old mattresses or sofas and even cars or wardrobes.

Modern legislation now deals with that kind of irresponsible behaviour but the Litter Act, which has been repealed and replaced by several up-to-date statutes, did cause some worries when it was first enacted. One was the custom of throwing confetti at weddings. The problem was that it was thrown from a place to which the public are entitled to have access without payment, i.e. the surrounds of the church or the churchyard or even beneath the lychgate, but if it was left outside the church after the wedding, then the ingredients of the offence were complete. If it was both thrown and left in the street, then of course, the offence was complete. To avoid a prosecution, one solution was to seek permission from the priest before throwing the confetti (i.e., the *proper authority* mentioned in the Act), throw it within the grounds of the church and then sweep it up afterwards. Not an easy task on a windy or wet day.

Events such as football matches, agricultural shows and race meetings which took place in the open air did not enter the realm of the Litter Act because people paid to enter those premises.

If they dropped litter in such places, no offence was committed and in any case the relevant authorities employed people to tidy up when members of the public had left.

It will be seen from the rules laid down by the Litter Act, which was still in force during the 1960s, that paper-chases could fall foul of the law. A man running along a public right of way such as a woodland footpath while tossing pieces of torn paper on to the ground, then leaving it behind, could certainly be accused of dropping litter and leaving it so as to deface a place in the open air. Before heading into Ashfordly, therefore, I refreshed my knowledge of the Litter Act by studying my *Moriarty's Police Law* book, and then sallied forth to discuss the matter with Sergeant Craddock. He listened and said,

'Well, PC Rhea, this is something of a conundrum, is it not? We don't want to be spoilsports. I believe this event dates back a long time, even into Victorian times, so it would be churlish of us to bring it to an ignominious end. Before I go and have words with the organizers, have you any thoughts about the best way to deal with this?'

'One solution is to use something other than pieces of paper,' I said, 'Something that will not detract from the countryside if it is dropped and left.'

'Like what, pray?'

'Flower petals, corn, rice . . .'

'Not very practical, PC Rhea, where would you get sufficient flower petals for one thing? And as for rice or corn, I am sure the local birds would have a great time pecking it up before the competitors got there . . . and besides, someone would have to carry a sackful around the course. Not an easy task, not easy at all.'

'No sergeant.'

'It seems to me,' he said. 'That I must explain the law to the organizers and leave the decision to them. I doubt if we would receive any complaints about litter. . . .'

'Except from our Mr Ashcroft, Sergeant. I get the feeling he will make sure he attends and that if litter is dropped, he will make the formal complaint.'

'In which case, PC Rhea, he will be the man whose name will be recorded as the one who got the paper-chase banned. I would not wish my name to enter local historical records as the man who banned it. So I will speak to the organizers and explain things to them, and I will mention Mr Ashcroft's role in all this, just for the record.'

'There might be another solution, Sergeant,' a thought suddenly occurred to me.

'Go on, PC Rhea, surprise me.'

'Suppose the entire course was on private land, not using any public roads, footpaths or rights of way, and the landowners agreed to pieces of paper being used to mark the course? And suppose those same landowners charged the Harriers for using their land, not a lot. Just one penny. The famous old peppercorn rent?'

'Go on, this sounds reasonable.'

'Well, there's nothing in the law to specify what level of

entrance fees are relevant. I believe that if all those ingredients are met, there will not be any breach of the law.'

'It is our duty to uphold the law, PC Rhea, not to find ways to circumvent it. But I like the idea and will suggest it to the organizers,' and he smiled.

And so it was that the annual Ashfordly Harriers paper-chase took place in Aidensfield with every inch of the route being on private land, and the Harriers Club paying one penny to each of the landowners through whose property they passed. I explained the law in great detail to Mr Ashcroft but I don't think he was very pleased. One thing really upset him – none of the landowners in question would allow him on to their land to see if any litter was being unlawfully deposited.

But the Litter Act heralded the decline of that sport. It's many years since I last knew of a paper-chase but today the countryside is still suffering from litter of all kinds which is thrown from cars and dropped by tourists.

Chapter 2

Some villages and small towns in England have managed to retain their stocks, pillories, whipping posts and lock-ups even if they have long ceased to be a means of punishment for minor wrongdoing. Now they are a form of tourist attraction – as indeed they were right from the beginning. When stocks were used to penalize minor offenders, for example, they had the benefit of the culprit sitting there with his legs locked in. Because he was unable to move away, he found himself the focus of some public entertainment, usually consisting of things like bad eggs, rotten fruit, vegetables or even dead cats being thrown at him.

Pillories were similarly used, except that the prisoner's hands and sometimes his head were locked in as he stood immobile before the crowd. At both the pillory and stocks, the resident villain could be bombarded with almost anything which came to hand and this was always regarded as jolly good sport and wonderful entertainment. It also enabled market stallholders and others to get rid of rotting produce in a relatively useful way.

Years ago, every self-respecting village had a set of stocks – those without were known as hamlets and no true community wanted such a lowly classification! Stocks became highly fashionable after 1405 when Parliament ordered every village to have a set because they regarded them as important in the prevention of crime and the punishment of offenders. So popular were they, that lords of the manor constructed their own portable sets of stocks with which to punish erring servants around their estates.

Stocks were perhaps the most widely used of a selection of temporary places of confinement. They boasted many benefits – they were easy and cheap to maintain, they required no supervisor to watch over the prisoner and they could accommodate short term offenders whose punishment was often little more than a few hours of public ridicule in the open air. Surviving examples can still be found in parts of Yorkshire – the Wensleydale village of Bainbridge has a fine set although few means of ancient punishment have survived in the North York Moors. I know of no pillories in the moors, nor indeed can I recall any surviving whipping posts; these were often erected outside court houses but I believe examples have survived in other parts of the country. The visitor with a sharp eye might identify such remnants even if they have since been utilized for different purposes.

One example of a dual-purpose structure is the village lock-up. These varied around the country in size, shape and stature; one at Lingfield in Surrey looks like a miniature church complete with tower while most were little more than stone-built shelters with a roof and a door, and usually just large enough to accommodate one person sitting down. Indeed, some of them doubled as well-covers which can't have been very comforting for the person inside, nor indeed for those who were obliged to drink the water!

It was a task of the local constable to look after the stocks, pillories and village lock-ups because it was also his duty to prevent a variety of unwelcome occurrences ranging from murder, bloodshed, theft, robbery and affray to a host of very minor offences.

He would place people in the stocks to teach them a lesson and make them an example to others. He had to prevent things like swearing, drunkenness and profanation of the Sabbath Day; he had to apprehend rogues and vagabonds and keep an eye open for other offenders who might include wandering minstrels, tinkers, pedlars or strolling players. Stocks and pillories were used in the short term to deal with a whole range of minor miscreants such as those who committed drunkenness, who sold under-weight bread, who used bad language or who committed any other kind of minor misdeed. Some early references to imprisonment usually meant a few hours in the stocks while regular offenders could be whipped – hence the whipping post. Persistent rogues and vagabonds could be whipped, for example, or even men and women convicted of stealing.

If someone committed a serious crime, say a murder, then the constable had to lock them up until the next visit by a travelling judge of assize or until a local justice gave some other instructions. For this, the village lock-up was used. This was more substantial than the stocks or pillory and a prisoner could spend some weeks in there. He could be released if someone paid a fine on his behalf or if his release was ordered by a magistrate but if he was locked up for a considerable period, then he had to be cared for, fed and supervized. That involved money and time – it meant someone had to be on duty all the time to watch over the prisoner. In some cases, prisoners were locked in these tiny places after they had been convicted in court; thus a village lock-up sometimes operated as a very modest local prison.

It follows that these lock-ups were sturdy places with very strong doors and secure locks, probably with no windows and certainly without comforts like heating, chairs or beds. They were primitive prisons in miniature but not every village had such a place. They might be located in small towns or in cities too but in rural areas, it was likely that several villages or parishes made use of the same lock-up. And, wherever they were, the task of looking after them and their inmates fell upon the local parish constable.

Looking back over history, the duties of a village constable in the 1960s were not greatly unlike those of eight hundred years earlier, although in modern times few rural police houses contained cells! Some did, so I am assured, but neither me, my wife nor my family would have welcomed a noisy, dirty and troublesome prisoner to share my hilltop home. Far better to take him to Ashfordly and even Eltering, there to languish in a cell in the police station until he could be dealt with.

In spite of much progress over the centuries, those ancient duties served to shape the work of the modern constable and I was to be reminded of this on a rare visit to Caldmoor, a remote and bleak place high among the heather above Ashfordly. Centuries ago, so the local history books claimed, there used to be a village at Caldmoor but as its name suggests, it is a cold and bleak location, many miles away from any other civilization. I believe the name comes from 'cold moor' but such was its isolation that it never attracted the interest of a landowner. Never was there a manor house at Caldmoor and so far as anyone could tell, it had been little more than a clutch of simple single-storey stone houses with ling (local heather) thatched roofs.

Their occupants had managed to wrest the toughest of livings from the inhospitable moorland with sheep farming their chief source of income. In the main, they tended moorland sheep from which they obtained wool which was later sold in the markets but some kept other livestock such as poultry or even sturdy hill cattle.

Over the years, people had left Caldmoor for easier work and better living conditions and by the end of the eighteenth or early nineteenth century, no one was living there. The sturdy squat houses with their curious roofs thatched with heather had gradually deteriorated into a state of disrepair as the savage wind and relentless weather had turned them into little more than piles of old stone. In some cases, even in the early twentieth century, chimney breasts could be seen, walls remained up to roof height and the shape of the houses could be discerned even though much of the fallen stone was by then smothered with heather. Now – apart from one curious building – there is nothing to see save the moorland sheep who live here and a few ridges of heather; beneath them, there will be the remnants of former walls but nothing else. It is an eerie place with a constant wind stirring the heather and little other noise save the cry of the curlew or the chatter of grouse, always angry at being disturbed. The location is still shown on maps, merely as the name of a lofty piece of moorland rather than a village, and the only access is via a long unmade moorland track although some public footpaths pass by.

Even until the 1960s, though, one building survived and it is still there. I think it survived due to its strong structure and the shape of its roof which is almost like a miniature cupola.

When I first set eyes on it, I thought it was the cover of a well. It is a sturdy building made from blocks of moorland granite and stands about eight feet high, narrowing slightly towards the top with a circular base some four feet in diameter. I am sure it must be of architectural interest because its domed roof is also fashioned from the same stone and it boasts a huge solid door with massive iron hinges and a formidable lock. In my time as the constable of Aidensfield, the door was always locked and so I never had the opportunity to peep inside. On its western side there was a small elongated but narrow gap between two stones, rather like the mouth of a pillar box – a window perhaps? Or a means of allowing air to penetrate this curious structure? Whatever its purpose, it was impossible to view the interior through it, it was too dark inside. From past research, I knew the people of Caldmoor had drawn their drinking water from a deep and very cool well somewhere on these moors, and I guessed this had been their well-cover, but I had never had cause to examine it closely and never found any explanation for its presence. Furthermore, I had no idea who owned it or who kept the key for I never had any cause to try and ascertain ownership. And so, from my point of view, that strange little domed building remained something of a puzzle; I saw it perhaps once every two or three years and each time wondered what it was and what it was doing in such a remote place, but in most cases, I forgot to delve into its past.

Then, one June morning just after nine o'clock, the police station at Ashfordly received a call to say that a rambler was missing on the moors. His name was Geoffrey Newcombe who was 57 years old and a civil engineer from Nottingham.

He was on a walking holiday on the moors but was travelling alone because his wife had died only a couple of months earlier; he'd told friends he wanted time by himself to come to terms with his grief and to walk in those places where they'd so enjoyed themselves over the years. Sensibly, he'd planned his route with stops at bed-and-breakfast places along the way and had provided a friend with an itinerary, just in case something went wrong – like falling and breaking his leg, or even getting lost! As an experienced rambler, however, no one thought he would get lost or come to any harm. By chance, I was in Ashfordly Police Station when the call came and I answered the phone.

'Hello,' said a distant voice. 'My name is Alan Russell, I'm ringing from Nottingham.'

I listened carefully as he expressed concern about his friend, Geoffrey Newcombe. It seemed Geoffrey had planned to walk across the moors on public footpaths, taking a week to do so and covering a modest distance each day. The day before yesterday, he'd stayed the night in Whemmelby and yesterday, he was going to walk from Whemmelby to Shelvingby which entailed crossing some of the highest and most remote parts of the moors. He'd told Alan Russell he expected to arrive in Shelvingby by nine o'clock in the evening at the latest, giving him the phone number of his lodgings. It was known that Geoffrey had been in Whemmelby as arranged but he had not arrived in Shelvingby at the expected time. He'd still not arrived by 11 p.m. when his friend rang and then, when Alan had rung the lodgings this morning, there was still no sign of him. Now it was time to become concerned.

'He's perfectly capable of coping out of doors for a night or two, especially in summer,' Alan Russell added. 'He's fully equipped, he always carries a small tent and provisions, and of course, he's a very experienced rambler. Normally, I'd not be concerned but he has been under some strain lately, with the death of his wife and problems at work, they're closing some of the offices where he works, and as I've heard nothing from him, I felt I had better report this.'

'He sounds very sensible,' I assured the caller. 'So what else have you done?'

'I rang the local hospitals and ambulance stations to see if there'd been some kind of emergency, but there hasn't. That's all I can tell you.'

Whilst I was speaking to Alan Russell and obtaining a list of Geoffrey's planned halts, I was checking his route on a map on the wall above the office telephone and could see there was a well defined public right of way across the moors between Whemmelby and Shelvingby. I confirmed this was the route Geoffrey was supposed to be following but it was entirely on high moorland with one or two marshy patches in hollows among the heather but with no villages between and only a handful of very isolated farmsteads anywhere near the track. It meant there were very few places to provide emergency help if he'd needed it although, to be fair, he was not entirely alone on those heights. At night, he'd have been able to see the farm lights in the darkness – but whether he'd been able to summon their help was another matter. One small problem was that some of those farms, I knew, did not have a telephone – they were too remote – but it was feasible he might have taken shelter in one of them without being able to notify anyone.

'Well, the good news is the weather's been fine and dry,

and we've had no reports of anyone being found ill or wandering, Mr Russell, but I have Geoffrey's route before me. It crosses some very remote and high moorland, with one or two farms along the way. Probably without telephones. He might be at one of them.'

'I hope so, I really do.'

'Look, give me your number, and the number of the lodgings he's heading for, and I'll pop out to check the area. I just hope he's not injured himself in some hidden gulley way off the beaten track, but if he does turn up, do ring us – please! If you can't raise anyone here at Ashfordly, ring Eltering Police and leave a message for me,' and I gave him the number. 'It's staffed twenty four hours a day but I'll warn Eltering of this before I leave here.'

And so it was that I decided to take the minivan on to that lofty area of moorland known as Caldmoor. I would park on the highest place I could find, bearing in mind the roughness of the moorland tracks, and would walk around the area to gain a broad view of any places he might be lying. I'd also take a pair of powerful binoculars to aid my search and would visit all the farms along his route even if it meant a walk of almost two miles in one case. I told the duty sergeant at Eltering where I was heading and why (Sergeant Craddock at Ashfordly was on his weekly rest day) and that I would be in radio contact should Geoffrey Newcombe turn up. I expressed a view that it was not yet necessary to call out a full search party or to alert the Moorland Rescue Team although that might be the next course of action if Geoffrey was not traced in the next few hours.

Although Sergeant Craddock was away, I was not acting sergeant in his absence – I had qualified for promotion but acting sergeants were utilized only if the current sergeant was absent for a prolonged period, say a period of annual leave, a week or more, or attending a course of some kind. The duty sergeant at Eltering, however, seemed happy to let me make my own decisions in this case. He did say, however, that if I needed assistance in the shape of extra constables to help in my own localized search, I should radio him without delay. I said I would first check at the farms along the route, and search portions of the route itself, because resorting to that action should establish whether or not we needed to extend our hunt. He agreed with that decision – both of us knew from experience that ramblers, either alone or in parties, regularly got behind schedule for various reasons, generally without any cause for alarm.

It took something like twenty-five minutes to drive from Ashfordly to the southern edge of Caldmoor with the road degenerating from a tarmac highway to an unmade track while all the time climbing gradually from the green lushness of the dale up to the bleakness of the exposed moorland. As I reached the higher stretches of the track, the squat shape of the cupola-topped mini-tower came into view and I decided it was a suitable place to park. Several dozen moorland sheep were dotted around the area but the ground near the little building was firm, much of it bearing signs of being regularly walked upon as ramblers came to inspect this odd little structure. There was clear evidence of them walking around it and peering through the slit-type window.

As I eased on to the sheep-shorn grassy patch, however, I thought I saw a movement at that tiny window. A bird perhaps? Some small animal which had clambered inside, like a stoat or a weasel? The door was closed, I noted, and there was no key in the lock. I'd never seen a key in that lock so it must be something fairly small to have squeezed through that slim gap. When I climbed out of the van, therefore, I decided to peep inside to see what it was but I got the shock of my life when I saw two eyes peering out at me. Human eyes.

I backed off in shock but quickly gathered my wits and peered again at the slit. There were definitely two eyes in there . . . and a person moving about.

'Geoffrey Newcombe?' I ventured, wondering how on earth he had come to be shut in here. Had the door been open? Had he stepped inside, only for the door to slam shut in the wind to lock him in?

'No,' said a young male voice. 'I'm Stuart Bailey.'

'What are you doing in there?' I felt a bit of a chump stooping down to talk to the gap in the wall. It was like talking to a pillar box and I was pleased there was no one around to witness this.

'Are you a policeman?' those eyes were peering intently at me now.

'Yes, I'm PC Rhea from Aidensfield.'

And with that, the eyes vanished as their owner ducked out of sight.

'Hello,' I called, moving closer. 'Hello, Stuart?'

There was no reply. The lad – for it was clearly a young lad probably in his early teens – was now squatting out of my vision and refusing to speak.

'Stuart?' I called. 'Look, I'm not going to harm you but if it's not a daft question, what are you doing in there?'

No reply. I called his name several times but he remained out of sight in the depths of the building and because he did not reply, I went to check the heavy door. It was firmly closed and locked but there was no key. Somebody had clearly shut the lad in here – a joke, no doubt. This was a midweek morning, though, when children should be at school but from only the briefest of glances, I was not sure whether this inmate was of school age. That one glance, quick thought it had been, suggested he was in his late teens. Probably he'd left school – or was about to do so this coming summer. Then I returned to the hole in the wall.

'Stuart, you're locked in. I can't open the door. Who did this?'

No reply.

'Was it some pals playing tricks? Where's the key? How long have you been here? If I had the key I could let you out . . . you can't be left in here . . . have you got the key? Did they leave it with you in there in case someone came along to let you out?'

No reply.

I was now in some kind of dilemma. I was searching for a missing rambler and instead had found a youth locked in what had become a miniature prison somewhere on the desolate moors. Clearly, someone had locked him in and equally clearly, that someone had gone away with the key. That meant there was a key. So who kept it? Someone who'd had it for years? On every occasion I'd been here, I'd never seen a key in the lock but there was no way I could smash down the door or open it.

I had no suitable tools and that door would defy the strongest of men and most powerful tools. Then, probably because this kid had been locked inside, I realized what this might have been years ago – a village lock-up! The sole remaining structure from the ancient village of Caldmoor . . . surely this demonstrated how impregnable it had been – and still was! The more I thought about that likelihood, the more feasible it became. Unless there was a well inside too?

Again, I tried talking through the slot.

'Look, Stuart, I have to go. I'm looking for a gentleman rambler who's lost or he could be hurt, I'm going to ask at the farms up here. I'm leaving my van where it is, just behind you, you can't see it from in there but I'll be back in a while. And if you're not out by the time I get back, I'll have to see about getting somebody to break that door down.'

'No, no, Mr Rhea, no don't do that . . . he'll come and let me out, you'll see, when he feels it's time. He wouldn't want you to damage this place, really he wouldn't.'

There was almost a hint of panic in his voice. For all the lad's anxiety, I was pleased I had got a response and now those dark eyes returned to the slot window.

'Who'll let you out?'

'My dad, he locked me in. He often does that.'

'Locks you in here?' I must have sounded horrified at the thought.

'When I do things wrong. He used to lock me in the cupboard under the stairs but now I'm too big he puts me in here.'

'How long for?'

'Depends, depends what I've done. An hour or two, half a day, depends. Sometimes he says he'll send for the police to take me away . . .'

'Which is why you tried to hide from me, eh?'

'Aye, well, I was a bit worried when you turned up. But when you said you was looking for that hiker chap, well I knew you hadn't come for me. So I'll just wait till dad comes for me, he's got a key, don't you worry about me. That hiker chap, well some hiker chap, it could be your feller, is at our house, turned his ankle last night. Not broke or owt like that, just twisted, went over on a loose rock, he said he'd be all right after a night's rest. He wanted to ring somebody up but we've no phone, Mr Rhea, not out here.'

'Well, it looks as though we might have found our missing man, thanks for that. I'll go to your farm and see what's happened to him. So what did you do to get yourself locked in here?'

'Left the hot tap running, Mr Rhea, ran all the hot water off . . . forgot to turn it off . . . dad was mighty cross about that. It takes ages for our fire to warm the water and now they'll have to light a fire in the daytime, not that it's very cold today but dad said it was a load of extra bother he could do without, so he wanted to teach me a lesson.'

'And has he?'

'Aye – till I do summat else daft,' he grinned.

'That's life, Stuart. So which is your farm?'

'North Ghyll Head,' he said. 'You can see the roof from here, blue slates.'

'I can see it,' I said, locating a spread just over the brim of the moor. 'Right, Stuart, I'm off. I'll be a while. Don't go away!'

'As if!' he laughed.

Due to the rough nature of the moorland, there was no way I could drive my low-slung van through the heather and so it meant a long walk. As I approached North Ghyll Head, Mrs Bailey spotted me striding across the farmyard and came out to greet me. When I mentioned a missing hiker, she knew immediately that the man in question was sitting in her lounge. She explained she'd not been able to inform anyone last night because her husband was out and she didn't drive, and the nearest phone box was six miles away. But she had tended to Mr Newcombe as if he was a cow with a strained leg.

'It was just a strain, Mr Rhea, nothing broken, I bound it with a cold wet bandage and made sure he rested it. I reckon he's fit to leave now, my husband said he'd take him down to Ashfordly by tractor when he's got his jobs done but that might not be till this afternoon.'

'Well, I've got my van parked near that lock-up, I can take him with me, if we can get him over to the van.'

'He might be able to walk now, I reckon he'll be on his feet anytime now and a spot of exercise will do him good. Come on through.'

Geoffrey Newcombe was a cheerful man with a ready smile; thick-set with a mop of unruly grey hair and bright blue eyes, he tried to get to his feet as I walked into the room but I told him not to try.

I explained why I was there and he apologized for the fuss he had created, but I said there was no real problem and that I was prepared to take him to Ashfordly or some other local village or inn until he could make his own arrangements to get home.

'I was heading for Gelderslack tonight, Mr Rhea, bed-and-breakfast at Rose Cottage, a Mr and Mrs Foster. That friend of mine, Alan, the one who rang you, well, he was going to come and collect me from there tomorrow morning, so if I can get to Gelderslack, I'll be fine.'

'I'll take you,' I said. 'All we have to do now is get you across the moor to my van. Can you walk that far?'

'I'm not sure, I don't want to damage my ankle, it could be rough underfoot out there.'

'I'll get our Harry to take you on his tractor, it'll only take a minute, he'll have time for that,' said Mrs Bailey. 'I'll fetch him, he's in the out-buildings.'

And so it was that I managed to locate the missing

rambler but as we chugged across the heather on the back of Harry Bailey's tractor, I knew I must query the matter of the lad in the old lock-up.

'Mr Bailey,' I shouted above the noise of the engine. 'That little building ahead of us. Is it the old lock-up?'

'Aye,' he said. 'It is.'

'Is there a well under it?'

'Nay, lad,' he shouted.

'And you have the key?'

'Aye, I have that. Been in my family for generations, it has, yon key.'

'Why is that?'

'Constables of Caldmoor we were. Go back nearly to the Conqueror they reckon, as constables. My ancestors built yon lock-up and cared for it, down the years. It belongs to our family. We saw to t'prisoners, fed 'em, maintained yon lock up. Even got locked up in there ourselves, most of us, well, most of the menfolk that is, down the years, for misbehaving. Put in there by our dads. I got locked in there whenever I misbehaved and so did my dad and his dad before him and his dad before him, as far back as you can go.'

'Like your Stuart?'

'Aye – oh, God, Mr Rhea! With all this going on this morning, I'd forgotten he was still in there. . . .'

'I talked to him, he doesn't seem worried about being there.'

'He spends a lot of time in there, Mr Rhea, just like I did and my dad before me, and it's done none of us any harm. Mebbe this time it'll teach him not to leave hot taps running. Anyway, I'll let him loose now and take him back with me.'

Geoffrey Newcombe was listening to these exchanges with clear bemusement but he made no comment, save to offer

Harry Bailey some cash for his overnight stay, care and food, but the farmer would have none of it.

'It's a bad day when you can't look after your fellow folks without wanting payment,' he grunted. 'I'm just glad you're no worse, Mr Newcombe.'

He dropped us near my waiting van and then turned his attention to the lock-up, opening the door with a huge key. Stuart, a small built lad about sixteen, staggered into the daylight, blinking against the brightness of the sun, then clambered on to the rear of the tractor without a word as his father secured what was in effect the family lock-up. I suppose it was somewhat unusual for a family to have its own lock-up in this way, and even more unusual to make use of it for its original purpose and although I wondered about the legality of locking-up a troublesome youth in such a place, I didn't think the lad would make an official complaint about it. He seemed to think it was quite a normal thing to happen to him if he misbehaved.

'Come along,' I said to Geoffrey Newcombe, 'Let's get you back to civilization.' And before setting off, I radioed Eltering Police Station to tell them Mr Newcombe had been found with only a slight injury and was now on his way to meet a friend. I did not mention the lad in the lock-up but must admit I wondered if Stuart Bailey, when he was fully grown, would continue the family tradition by locking up any of his own youngsters if they transgressed.

Whatever its future, the Baileys had a very useful lock-up which could be hired for almost any legal purpose. A private prison in fact. I wondered if the idea of private prisons might eventually receive official approval.

If Caldmoor is a remote part of the North York Moors, the

same can be said of Geldersdale except that the latter is a deep and uninhabited valley, at the lower end of which, albeit on a nearby hill, stands the hamlet of Gelderslack.

If one stands looking to the east at the famous Surprise View which features in tourist information leaflets about Gelderslack and the surrounding district, then Geldersdale lies to one's left, i.e. the north. It is a lush steep-sided valley containing Geldersbeck, a small stream which rises on the moors above, and for almost its entire length of five miles, the little dale is densely wooded with deciduous trees. The dale is known for its display of wild daffodils in the spring and there is a public footpath beside the beck, taking hikers from Gelderslack up to the wild moors to the north via the rather rocky dale head. Not surprisingly, the route through Geldersdale is very popular with the few ramblers who are aware of its location but it is also known to ornithologists for its bird life and botanists for its variety of wild plants. Some say Geldersdale is one of the best kept secrets of the moors because it does not attract bus loads of tourists or hordes of motorists; there is little doubt that those who enjoy and respect the quiet dale are true connoisseurs of the countryside.

Among its hidden gems is a solitary but very atmospheric old building. It is a squat stone church which dates to Norman times and which has an apsidal crypt from the same period, *c.* 1087. The church is dedicated to St Withberga and can accommodate only about thirty people sitting down; really, it is a church in miniature and although it was a Catholic church until the Reformation, it is now Anglican and used only occasionally for special services. One of them is held on St Withberga's Feast Day which is 8th July, and there may be events like carol services at

Christmas or perhaps a harvest festival.

From time to time, the old crypt, which is a church in its own right reached by a stone staircase from the main aisle above, is also used although this is now featured more as a tourist attraction. Not many small churches have such a crypt; with its stone floor, arched interior and solid stone altar with tiny windows facing east in its curved wall, it is a most interesting place, a complete survival from the time of William the Conqueror. Down the centuries, there have been few alterations to this church, although a tiny bell tower was added in the fourteenth century – it boasts just one bell. It seems this was never a parish church and may have been more of a chapel in the moors for the use of travelling priests or monks, but it stands today as a true gem in its lonely woodland setting. It is about a mile and a half from Gelderslack.

On a Saturday in July, a small party of three people decided to walk the route which passed through Geldersdale. They were all in their early sixties – two ladies and a gentleman (a man and his wife, and her sister) – and their walk was more of a stroll in the countryside than a hike, although they did come down from the moors, having caught a bus to a point a couple of miles north. Their purpose was to cross the moor to the dale head via a public footpath, then walk down Geldersdale and into the village of Gelderslack where they would have afternoon tea. They would then catch a bus back to Eltering. A nice afternoon's outing with a modest but bracing walk.

They were Philip and Doreen Ostler, with Doreen's sister, Grace Marchant, who was a widow, all of whom lived in Eltering. They were nice people, very fit and agile for their age and they loved to explore the countryside around them.

And so it was that they came down from the moors, successfully negotiating the rocky path at the dale head to find themselves walking beside the stream which flowed down Geldersdale. It was about five o'clock in the afternoon of that Saturday when they came upon St Withberga's little church on its beautiful but lonely site beside Geldersbeck. As one might expect, they popped in to have a look around. It seems they were totally captivated by the little church and quite stunned by the ancient crypt with its historic background. They all descended into the crypt and examined its contents, then, being regular churchgoing people, decided to kneel before the stone altar for a few minutes of personal prayer. In complete silence, therefore, they bowed their heads for about five minutes.

It was perhaps unfortunate that their moments of silent prayer coincided with the daily visit by the custodian of the church, a man called Ralph Chambers who was also a churchwarden for the parish church in Gelderslack. Ralph's duty was to open the huge studded door of St Withberga's at nine each morning and lock it again at five each evening. He coincided those trips with walking his two golden retriever dogs, covering some of the route on his bicycle and walking the final few hundred yards.

When he arrived at St Withberga's, therefore, he found the door standing open as he had left it that morning, popped his head into the church, saw it was empty but listened for sounds of people who may still be present in the crypt. The sound of their voices and footsteps could always be heard from down there, the noise being amplified by the ancient stones as it rose into the nave.

He heard nothing, assumed there was no one in the crypt and left, closing the door and locking it. And off he went with his dogs, back to Gelderslack.

Philip, Doreen and Grace, with their heads bowed in prayer, heard the door close but thought little about it, thinking it might be other visitors moving around or someone tidily closing the door which they had found standing open. And so, for a few minutes, they were unaware of their plight. It was only when they retraced their steps back up to the nave and tried to leave, that they realized the door was locked. For a moment or two, they thought it might have blown shut in the wind or that others visitors had closed it, but when Philip tried to pull it open he realized it would not move. No amount of jiggling with the sneck had any effect; with a sinking heart, he realized it was locked. They were locked in and there was no way out.

He did the first thing that came into his mind. He shouted while hammering on the door with his fist. The combined noises should alert the person who had done this, and who shouldn't be far away. After all, the door can't have been closed for long . . . they hadn't been in the crypt more than ten minutes in total. But ten minutes was long enough for Ralph to walk the few hundred yards to his bike, mount it and ride off. In a few moments, he was too far away to hear any shouting or banging.

Inside the church, Philip Ostler did his best not to panic; he told his lady companions that he felt sure someone would come past the church and hear them, and then raise the alarm. But no one came. Or if they did, they did not hear Philip's distress calls.

And so they sat in the pews and prayed for deliverance, with Philip returning to the door from time to time to hammer upon it and shout anew. Who would know they were here? They'd not told anyone where they were going

. . . and was the church open on Sundays? It wasn't used for regular services. How long would they have to remain here?

It didn't take many minutes for Grace Marchant to dissolve into near panic and Philip knew that the fate of them all rested with him. But they were in the wilds of the moors, deep in a remote but beautiful dale and it was Saturday evening . . .

Then Philip had a bright idea. He knew how, down the ages, church bells had been rung to raise the alarm if an enemy invasion was imminent, or to warn of a curfew, or to celebrate weddings and honour funerals. And this lonely little church possessed a solitary bell but did it work? And if so, would anyone hear it? He went to the rear of the nave and saw the bell rope which had been lifted and tied to the wall at a height to prevent visitors pulling it for no reason, but by hauling one of the pews to a point below it he could stand on it and reach the rope. And, with some considerable effort, he freed the rope and began to ring the bell. It was a tinny sound, the clapper moving instead of the bell itself, but it was producing considerable noise and all he could do now was hope.

And that is where I came into the story. By chance I was in Gelderslack, looking for Ralph Chambers. He had witnessed a traffic accident in Eltering during the week and had given his name and address to both drivers; my task was to obtain a written witness statement from him so that I could complete my accident report.

When I arrived at his home I was told, 'He's just gone to lock the old church, Mr Rhea, he should be back any minute now. You'll catch him coming up Surprise View bank.'

I decided to wait at the top of Surprise View bank just in

case Ralph decided to go somewhere else before returning home; that way, I could be sure of catching him. And as I waited on the summit, I saw him pushing his bicycle up the hill and almost simultaneously, heard the sound of a church bell. I found it rather puzzling because it was not Sunday, there was no services on a Saturday tea-time – at least none of which I was aware – and this did not sound anything like a bell-ringing practice. It was more like children messing about, being merely the sound of a single bell coming from somewhere. And I had no idea where the noise was coming from.

'Now then, Mr Rhea,' said Ralph as he halted at my side, panting with the exertion. He was in his late sixties, I guessed, a sturdy countryman who worked for the Forestry Commission. He was one of those people who seemed to perform every necessary chore in a small village. 'Are you waiting for me?'

'I am, Ralph, it's about that accident you witnessed.'

'Right, well, you'd better come to my house and I'll tell you what happened.'

'Before we go, Ralph, what bell is that?' It was still ringing somewhere in the distance, not regular strokes but very spasmodic. I raised my hand to indicate the general direction of the sound.

'What bell?' he frowned and I realized his hearing was perhaps not as good as it should be.

'There's a church bell,' I said, pointing towards the dale. 'Somewhere over there, a single bell, it's been ringing on and off for the last few minutes.'

'I can't hear a bell,' he cocked his head on one side. 'Are you sure?'

'I am, I can hear it now. I'm sure it's coming from that

direction, it sounds like a bell in Geldersdale to me,' I had to tell him.

'Well, t'only church in those parts is St Withberga's, and I've just come from there. Locked it for t'night.'

'Well, the bell can't ring by itself,' I laughed, then jokingly added, 'You haven't locked somebody in, have you?'

I could see that I had probably hit the right target. The frown of uncertainty which crossed his face said a great deal. 'You know, Mr Rhea, I might well have done that! I thought it was empty but mebbe somebody was in the crypt . . . if they were, they were very quiet when I was there, that's all I can say.'

'Could it be somebody in distress?' That thought now crossed my mind. 'Somebody in need of help perhaps? Can that bell be rung when the church is locked?'

'Only by somebody climbing up the outside of the church and I doubt if they'd manage that without a ladder, Mr Rhea. Or throwing stones at it. Whatever it is, I'd best get back to have a look. It's a good job you heard yon bell, I'd never have heard it.'

'I've got my van just round the corner, I'll run you back,' I offered. 'If somebody is hurt, they might need a lift.'

And so I gave Ralph a lift along the Geldersdale path as far as the van could take us, and then we got out to walk the final few hundred yards.

'I can hear it now,' he said as we drew closer. 'It's definitely St Withberga's.'

'It's the SOS message,' I told him. 'Listen – there's three long rings, well, three rings with a long gap between each one, three short ones and another three long ones, and then a long pause before it starts again.'

And so it was that we rescued three very worried people.

Ralph could not apologize enough to them but as we all walked together back towards my waiting van, I made him promise he'd physically check the crypt before locking up for the night. He assured me he would – and he also said he'd visit his doctor for a hearing test.

Chapter 3

Even in modern times, many people indulge in superstitious behaviour as a means of ensuring good fortune, happiness and health or merely in the hope of meeting the right romantic person. In thinking rationally about these practices, the whole idea of superstition is rather ridiculous, nonetheless we've all got our little private customs and foibles by which we hope to ensure a happy path through life, even if we never really consider precisely why we adopt such practices. But even if we try to consider those practices in a rational way, we continue to live by them just in case things go wrong if we don't!

Examples include wearing lucky clothes when going for an interview for a job, keeping lucky symbols which might vary from a rabbit's foot to a particularly lovable soft toy, nailing a horseshoe to the house door or outbuilding, crossing our fingers, touching wood, never having thirteen at table or not having our homes numbered thirteen, never leaving the house by the same door as one used for entry (or always using the same one, depending where you live) or shouting 'rabbits' several times on the first day of the month. We think we will be lucky if we see a pair of magpies, a chimney sweep or a black cat but we feel unlucky if a picture falls from its hook on the wall or if someone spills salt or if we inadvertently walk under a ladder. Some ladies will never have snowdrops or pictures of robins in the house in case they attract ill fortune, some will never take red and white flowers into a hospital but most of us take greenery indoors at Christmas because we think it brings good fortune in the year to come.

A good example of our adherence to superstition was a man who said to me, 'I don't believe in superstitions, but would never have thirteen at my dinner table.' The same man would say 'fingers crossed' if he was embarking on something that required a spot of luck, like selecting a tombola ticket or posting his football pools coupon.

Little Miss Murfitt, a mature lady of uncertain years who lived at Horseshoe Cottage in Aidensfield, was another such person. With a name like that, it was inevitable she would be nicknamed Miss Muffit and teased about sitting on a tuffet or being frightened by a spider but in fact she was a very tiny person. Scarcely five feet tall and extremely minute in every sense (she wore children's clothes and shoes, for example), she rode around on a small pint-sized bicycle with a basket on the front. She was retired, having owned a shop in Ashfordly which specialized in things required by knitters and needlewomen. When she ran her shop, she had a small ladder which she found necessary to reach the higher shelves and stacks of drawers laden with knitting patterns, cotton reels or balls of wool, but it was a successful business and when she sold it, she was able to retire in comfort. She did not take a great part in the social life of the village but, when asked, would cheerfully help at things like garden fêtes, whist drives, money-raising charity events and local concerts. For all her business success, however, she was highly superstitious.

Apart from having numerous horseshoes nailed to her walls and doors, she had a houseleek growing on her roof to stop the house catching fire and a rowan tree in her garden which protected the house and its owner against almost everything which was remotely nasty such as disease, ill fortune, bad weather and even the Evil Eye.

She would never open her umbrella in the house and had an ancient hot cross bun hanging in her scullery to ensure good fortune throughout the year, and to guard the house against fire. She had an encyclopedic memory for luck-bringing superstitions which she carried out all day and every day, and although she had been successful in business, she was yet to meet Mr Right in spite of being nearly seventy. Her luck in business did not seem to extend into her private life because she never seemed to win raffle prizes or enjoy greater good fortune than the rest of us.

Nonetheless she kept trying and her persistence was successful when she won a box of chocolates in the annual Christmas draw at the village pub. Every year, the pub staged a mighty raffle in aid of orphans and sick children; it was always a success and generated lots of freely given prizes ranging from turkeys to Christmas puddings via a whole range of useful and not-so-useful prizes. Sales of tickets guaranteed a very handsome donation to the charity. Nonetheless, not many people would welcome the prize of a six week old piglet, for example, or a lorry load of manure, or six pullets on the point of lay but the thought was there and they could always swop such prizes for something else if they happened to win. And so it was that Miss Murfitt bought a book of twenty tickets for £1 to find herself with a winner among them. To the cheers of the assembled crowd on that Friday before Christmas, she endured the walk up to the bar where Oscar Blaketon presented her with her prize.

'Oh, I'm so so lucky!' she simpered. 'I knew my luck would turn one day . . .'

When she got home with her box of chocolates, however, she found herself much luckier than she had realized.

That night in the peace and cosiness of her little cottage, and before going to bed, she removed the brown paper wrapping in which it was firmly wrapped. It bore the words in ink 'Box of Chocolates – Raffle Prize' on the top. She threw it on to the dying embers of her fire and opened the box to sample the first of its contents. She was stunned to find £100 in crisp £5 notes tucked inside. The money was neatly arranged on top of the uppermost layer of chocolates and was eminently visible upon opening the lid but there was no note to explain its presence. Most certainly when the list of prizes had been mentioned, there had been no reference to a prize of £100, whether contained in a box of chocolates or not. Surely there would have been if the money had been intended as a prize? This now placed her in a dilemma. Was the money really intended as a prize or not? Or had someone placed it there temporarily as a place of safe keeping, only to forget about it when donating the box to the raffle? But she hadn't read or heard of anyone misplacing such a large amount of money – after all, it was more than a month's wages for most of the local men. Filled with doubt as to the correct thing to do, she replaced the chocolate and closed the lid of the box. Tomorrow, she would speak to Oscar Blaketon about it. Being a former police sergeant as well as the man who had organized the raffle and presented the prizes, he would know the right thing to do. He might even recall the name of person who had donated the chocolates in which case Miss Murfitt could discuss it with that person.

At nine thirty next morning, Saturday, she arrived at the inn clutching the box of chocolates and went in to find Blaketon preparing for opening at 10.30 a.m.

The famous Aidensfield fire was blazing in the grate and he was humming a tuneless piece of music as he busied himself stocking the bar.

'Ah, Miss Murfitt!' he smiled a welcome. 'This is a rather early visit, we're not open yet for serving drinks. Oh, I see you've brought the chocolates back. Some kind of problem, is there?'

'Oh, it's not really a problem, Mr Blaketon, there's nothing wrong with the chocolates if that's what you're thinking,' she smiled as she put the box on the bar counter. 'In fact, it might not be a problem at all but I thought it was something I should mention to you.'

'Well, I'm all ears,' he grinned.

'Just open the box, Mr Blaketon,' she challenged him with a smile which suggested some kind of mystery.

'It's not a trick box, is it? Filled with something that jumps out when I open the lid?'

'No, nothing like that. Go on, have a look. You gave it to me . . .'

His face now developed a look of deep apprehension as he wondered what lay in store for him if he dared to lift that lid but, with little Miss Murfitt standing there with her chin barely above the level of the counter, he took a deep breath and did as she asked.

'Good grief! Money!' he cried. 'How much is there?'

'A hundred pounds, all in five pound notes,' she said.

'So why are you showing me this, Miss Murfitt?'

'It was in the box last night when I opened it. The list of prizes said nothing about winning £100 so I'm not sure I'm really entitled to it. I came to ask your advice.'

'Well, blow me! I don't know what to say. You're very honest, though, I'll grant you that. But I can assure you there was no mention of a cash prize of that amount. So far as we were concerned, it was just a box of chocolates, a very normal sort of raffle prize. I remember when it was handed to us for the raffle it was neatly wrapped in brown paper with a note to say what was inside, so if the money was in there when you won it, then I suppose it must be yours to keep.'

'Oh, but I couldn't, Mr Blaketon. I might not be entitled to it, I can't honestly imagine anyone putting that amount of money into a box of chocolates, then giving it away for a raffle prize, not without saying.'

'Well, I can tell you we've had no calls about it, that box was here a couple of weeks ago, along with lots of other prizes, so if someone has made a mistake you'd think I'd have been contacted before now.'

'So what do you think I can do?'

'Well, one course, I suppose, is to report it to PC Rhea who will record it in his Found Property register, and if it's not claimed in three months it will become your property. That would establish your innocence if anyone reported it missing or even made a complaint about it being stolen.'

'Yes, I had thought about doing that but I wondered if you knew who had donated the chocolates? I could have a word with them first perhaps, to see if it belonged to them.'

'You could do that but if I were you, I'd tell PC Rhea

first. If you go and tell someone else what you've found, they might wrongly claim it as theirs! I think notifying the police is the best thing to do in the circumstances.'

'Yes, yes, I can see what you mean. Thank you, Mr Blaketon, I wouldn't want this money to get into the wrong hands.'

Which is how I came to be involved in this saga.

When Miss Murfitt arrived at my police house with the box of chocolates in the basket of her bicycle, I was off duty, cleaning my private car. I saw her lean the bike against our gatepost and then, somewhat hesitantly, approach me while clutching the precious box.

'Good morning, Miss Murfitt,' I smiled. Everyone called her Miss Murfitt. I suppose she had a Christian name but no one ever used it – and probably had no idea what it was. 'How can I help you?'

'I don't want to be a nuisance, PC Rhea,' she said, eyeing my as I clutched the wash leather which I was using to polish the car. 'I can see you are not on duty this morning . . .'

'I'm working this evening,' I said. 'But there's no problem. How can I help you?'

And so she explained about winning the box of Cadbury's Dairy Milk with the £100 inside. She showed me the box with its decorative lid and opened it to reveal the twenty £5 notes.

'Mr Blaketon said I should report it to you, Mr Rhea, so that it is shown in police records, as found property.'

'Yes, that seems a good idea. I'll record it, but you can keep the money and if it's not claimed in three months, then it is yours. But if you won it in a raffle prize which was securely wrapped as you say, then I would consider it is yours anyway. It's been legitimately acquired and I can confirm no one's reported it lost or stolen.'

'Don't you think we should try to find out who it belongs to?' she was clearly concerned. 'Mr Blaketon was clearly worried that if I started asking who had donated the chocolates with my reason for asking, then someone might make a dishonest claim to the money.'

'He's right, Miss Murfitt. I think the fewer people who know about this, the better. Leave it with me. I'll have words with Oscar Blaketon when I'm on duty this evening and I'll see if I can track down the donor. I'll keep you informed – but in the meantime, keep the money in a safe place and if it's not claimed in three months, then it will be yours anyway. I'll make sure it goes into our Found Property Register under your name.'

'Will it be all right for me to deposit the money in the bank? I wouldn't like such a large sum lying about the house.'

'Yes, and if anyone comes to claim it, you can either give them a cheque or draw out the money.'

'Thank you, Mr Rhea, I'll do as you suggest. I would hate someone to have the misfortune to lose such a lot of money due to my good fortune. You will keep me informed?'

'I will,' I promised. When she left on her tiny bicycle, I went into my office, made a note of the finding of £100 by Miss Murfitt and returned to my car washing duties.

I came on duty at 6 p.m. to work a 6 p.m.–2 a.m. shift; being Saturday night, it meant I could patrol the pubs and clubs in Ashfordly, Brantsford and district in the hope my uniformed presence would deter drunks, vandals and trouble-makers. My first call, however, was on Oscar Blaketon. When I went into the pub, it was deserted even though it was officially open and for that, I was pleased. My modest enquiry would not be overheard. I explained that I was going to try and trace the original owner of the £100 in Miss Murfitt's chocolate box whereupon Blaketon said,

'I didn't give her the donor's name, Nick, but it was Bessy Sampson.'

'You mean *the* Bessy Sampson?'

The Sampsons were a family of troublemakers and small-time crooks who lived on a council estate in Ashfordly; Bessy's husband, Jack, was always in bother either being drunk, fighting and acts of petty violence against things like traffic lights, shop windows and car head-lights. He did a lot of kicking when he was in drink and seemed to like the sound of breaking glass.

'Don't sound so surprised, Nick. I'm well aware of the family's reputation but Bessy has a soft spot for children who are orphaned or neglected, she can be very charitable when she wants, or when she had any spare money. She called in one day and gave me that box of chocolates. It was wrapped up in brown paper, sealed with Sellotape and it had the words 'Box of chocolates' on the outside. I don't think she put the money inside, Nick; I reckon she just passed the chocolates on. She might have won them herself, or been given them by somebody. Now you know why I didn't tell Miss Murfitt where they'd come from. If Jack had known there was £100 in that box, he would claimed it like a shot! Bessy works in the Red Lion in Ashfordly, by the way, behind the bar. You might see her there if you're patrolling tonight.'

I made a special effort to pay an official visit to the Red Lion as early as possible so that I could have a quiet chat with Bessy, whom I knew by sight. She was a large and cheerful woman in her mid thirties who seemed to shrug off her husband's loutish behaviour as if he was little more than a mischievous child. She was behind the bar when I walked into the Red Lion; it was very early in the evening and four young men were playing darts at the far end of the bar but there was no one else in just yet.

'Hello, Mr Rhea, an early call is it?' she beamed one of her wide smiles.

'Just calling, Bessy, I wanted a quick word.'

'Not our Jack again, is it?'

'No,' I laughed. 'Not this time. Look, a quick question. Did you give a box of chocolates for a raffle at Aidensfield, the children's charity fund raising event?'

'Yes, I did. Nothing wrong, is there?'

'Nothing at all, Bessy but can I ask where you got it from?'

'It's not nicked, is it? Not our Jack?'

'No, nothing like that. I just wondered where you got it from.'

'Won it, didn't I? Here at work. We had a raffle to raise money for that jockey who fell off at Wetherby, going over those jumps. I won that box of chococates but nobody in our house likes chocolate so I passed it on to Aidensfield.'

'Was it wrapped when you won it?'

'It was, in brown paper with the words "box of chocolates" on the outside. That's how I knew what it was. I never opened it, Mr Rhea, just passed it on.'

'So who gave it for your raffle?'

'One of the regulars. I don't know his surname but everybody calls him Shorty. I think he was a jockey or stable lad years ago, which is why he supported our raffle. Look, what's all this about?'

'Let's just say I'm trying to trace the origin of that box of chocolates, just out of curiosity. There's no crime, no one's in bother, it's not a crime I'm trying to solve, it's just idle curiosity on my part and nothing official or criminal or illegal. When I find out who gave it originally, then I'll explain what all this is about. Meanwhile, we'll regard it as a bit of a mystery. How's that?'

'You mean people have kept winning it and passing it on for another raffle, nobody's got round to opening it?'

'Spot on, Bessy! So where can I find Shorty?'

'He'll be in tonight, Mr Rhea, bang at half-past eight. He always comes in then for his couple of pints.'

'I'll call and see him – but keep this as a surprise. You can listen to what he says . . . we might both learn something!'

Shorty was a stocky unshaven man with straggly ginger hair and although he might have once been a jockey, now he was thick-set and in my opinion looked far too heavy and much too old even to climb on board a horse. When I explained the edited version of the chocolate box mystery, he frowned and said, 'It was given to my missus, Mr Rhea, our neighbours gave it to us, for the raffle.'

'Already wrapped, was it?'

'Oh, aye, all nicely done up in brown paper with "box of chocolates" written on it. She asked if I'd hand it to the raffle organizers, so I did. That's all I can tell you about it.'

'I'd like a chat with your neighbour,' I said, assuring him there was no crime or suspicious behaviour to worry me. 'I'm just anxious to find out where the chocolates came from. It seems they've been passed from friend to friend.'

'Well, you can have a chat with her, Mr Rhea, she's Rita Scott and she lives in Albany Terrace, number seventeen. Tell her I sent you.'

At this development, Bessy chipped in with, 'Mr Rhea's hot on the trail of the box of chocolates, Shorty. We think it must have been given specially for raffles, nobody seems to have owned it!'

And so it was that I found myself knocking on Rita Scott's door. The brick-built terrace house was badly in need of a coat of paint and the thin curtains in the street windows next to it suggested the occupants did not have much spare money. When Rita opened the door, I saw she was an attractive young woman with a host of children hanging on to her apron but when she saw the uniform, her mouth dropped open. She looked terrified.

'Sorry to call on you like this,' I apologized and immediately wondered if I had interrupted her children's bedtime routine. 'Shorty said you wouldn't mind if I called.'

'Oh God, what's happened!' she cried, putting a hand to her mouth. 'Is it dad?'

'No, nothing like that, it's not trouble, Mrs Scott, it's just a rather silly enquiry.'

'Oh?' and she frowned heavily, as if not really believing that a policeman was on a mission that did not herald trouble.

'I'm trying to track down a box of chocolates which was won in a raffle at the Red Lion – it's not a case of trouble, I can assure you. Just curiosity on my part. Shorty says you gave it as a prize when they were trying to raise funds for a jockey who'd taken a nasty fall.'

'Oh, yes, right, yes. I did. He was asking for prizes and I had that box, unopened because I kept it out of the kids' sight. I thought it was a good cause and hadn't anything else in the house so I gave it to him. He said it would be a nice prize, boxes of chocolates are always nice to win.'

The thought flashed through my mind that this young woman and her family could benefit greatly from £100 and it was clear she had no idea of the box's contents.

'Was it wrapped up when you gave it to him?'

'Yes, in brown paper with a note on the outside to say what it contained. It was like that when my husband brought it home. He's a van driver.'

'The trail continues!' I laughed. 'So where did he get it from? Any idea?'

'Yes, he helped a motorist who'd got a puncture. It was a woman, quite elderly, he told me, and she couldn't jack up her car to get the wheel off so he stopped on the road to help her. Somewhere on the moors near Aidensfield, he said. He took her and the wheel to a garage to get the puncture mended. She was most grateful for his help and offered him some money but he refused, so she gave him that box of chocolates as a thank-you. She insisted he took it.'

'So you know my next question! Any idea who she was?'

'No, she was a visitor. From the Cotswolds, she said, she'd come to Yorkshire to see Ryedale because the houses and scenery are very like the Cotswolds. She was alone and had a car. She never gave him her name or anything. Just that box of chocolates. He never saw her again. He's in the house, if you want a word with him.'

I had a brief chat with her husband whose name was Paul, and he confirmed her story. He had no idea who the woman was or where she lived, but I did establish that the box was wrapped in brown paper when she handed it over to him. It would be about six or seven months ago, he added. I told the Scotts I would get in touch with them if and when the mystery was ever solved.

And there the trail ended.

A couple of days later, I went to see Miss Murfitt and gave her an account of my enquiries while voicing my belief that if the box of chocolates had originated somewhere in the Cotswolds after which it had followed a strange route of being repeatedly being donated as a raffle prize in Yorkshire, it was highly unlikely anyone would now make a claim for the money. Whatever the story behind the £100 cash, it now seemed as if the originator would never be traced. That being so, Miss Murfitt was quite entitled to keep it. When I told her that, she expressed her sincere belief that she had been a very lucky person which she felt was entirely due to her many personal procedures for bringing good fortune, but I did suggest she waited for the full three months as our Found Property procedures demanded.

I must admit I wondered if some generous person had given the money as a Christmas or birthday surprise to a friend or family member – and I guessed that that lucky (or luckless) person had never opened the box and had missed finding the treasure. If that was the case, then the recipient of the chocolates perhaps deserved to lose the windfall, but someone, somewhere, must have been wondering why he or she had never been adequately thanked for a very handsome present.

Miss Murfitt waited patiently for the required three months but no one came forward to report losing the £100. She did not keep it, however; she gave it to the children's charity for which that particular raffle had been organized, thus transferring her good fortune to someone more worthy to receive such unexpected funds. Following all this, and as a matter of courtesy, I told everyone involved in that chain of events, giving them a full account of the drama and advising them of the destination of the cash. Each was shocked at the thought of overlooking such a valuable gift but each assured me they would always open presents or prizes of boxes of chocolates in the future.

If some people are blessed with good fortune throughout their lives, then others are plagued with bad luck. In some cases, bad luck appears to follow them whatever they do and where ever they go. It matters not that they adopt the tactics of Miss Murfitt in trying to thwart their ill fortune – no amount of rabbits' feet, horseshoes, touched wood or crossed fingers seems to make the slightest difference. Things always seem to go wrong.

Such a man was Jeremy Flanders, a self-employed painter and decorator who lived in Aidensfield. He was a cheerful character of some forty-five years of age; married with a nice wife called Elizabeth and two teenage children, he had a round face, curly fair hair and a sturdy build. In his white paint-stained overalls, he looked very efficient, capable and helpful – which he was. Jeremy was a familiar sight in Aidensfield and district, usually up a ladder or decorating someone's front room.

It was perhaps fortunate that the bad luck he experienced did not transfer itself to his customers, otherwise he might have had difficulty persuading people to employ him. Whatever went wrong in his life was invariably something personal but more often than not, such disasters were of a very minor nature, usually more troublesome than dangerous, although he'd had some remarkable escapes. One example was when a sycamore tree blew down in a gale and just missed his workshop. It smashed his garden fence, demolished his compost heap and flattened his patch of new potatoes but Jeremy considered himself lucky because it missed the house, missed his workshop and missed his van.

There was the famous occasion when he forgot to post his football pools coupon – and checked it to find he'd have won £23,500; another time he took the family on holiday in a caravan at Skegness and they'd all gone down to the seafront when the gas cylinder blew up and destroyed it. Again, he thought he was lucky, especially as he'd merely rented the van. On another occasion, the strap of his watch broke and he lost it down a drain in the high street, only to be thwarted in a search because a flash flood occurred and swept it to heaven-knows-where. Once, when decorating an upstairs window at a house, a seagull flew overhead and he looked up to watch it – only to be bombed in the face by the contents of the gull's intestines and on another occasion the brakes of his van failed in the middle of Ashfordly and he had to drive into a wall to bring his vehicle to a shuddering halt. The snag was he also knocked the wall down.

I do not know the full extent of Jeremy's bad luck experiences but I believe his domestic life was beset with countless small troubles, like losing his van keys, leaving the bath water to overflow while he answered the phone, locking himself out of the house, letting the chip pan catch fire, forgetting to refill his private car with petrol and then running out on holiday, forgetting his wife's birthday and his wedding anniversary, forgetting to collect his mother-in-law from the bus station when she came to visit them and turning up on the wrong night at a friend's house for a party. Some might argue that this kind of mishap was not due to bad fortune; rather, it was a case of being disorganized or careless but Jeremy thought it was all due to bad luck. He did emulate Miss Murfitt by hanging a horseshoe on the wall of the house and someone even said he'd taken to carrying a rabbit's foot everywhere. But still the mishaps continued.

The day after getting the rabbit's foot, for example, he parked his van on a slope in Ashfordly while he carried out the painting of a shop front. His van was safely and properly parked beside the pavement as he carried out his work only feet away – but someone further up the street forgot to set the handbrake of their car. It rolled away and ran slap-bang into the rear of Jeremy's van, pushing it down the slope and into the rear of another car. Jeremy thought he was lucky because no one was injured. He said the same about the capsizing of the ferry he was supposed to use to cross the English Channel for a motoring holiday in France, the first family trip overseas. Happily, he and his family were not on board – they should have boarded two days later, but they might have been lost. Again, he thought he was lucky.

For all his misfortune, Jeremy was an affable character who was liked and trusted by everyone; he would do anything to help other people and disliked being a nuisance. Even when disaster struck, he maintained a cheerful face – perhaps he had learned not to become depressed by his apparent ability to attract misfortune.

When he tripped and fell heavily while coming downstairs one morning, therefore, he did not make too much of a fuss even though his foot hurt with eye-watering pain. He sat dazed on the bottom step, drawing his breath and clenching his teeth as he knew that something serious was wrong. Gingerly, he touched his ankle – the left one – but the pain made him winch and shout out. Elizabeth had heard the unusual noises, the bumping and shouting, and came running from the kitchen to see what had happened.

'What have you done?' there was clear alarm in her voice at the sight of Jeremy sitting and sighing with an ankle which looked to be held in a most awkward position.

'I tripped, up there,' he indicated the top of the stairs with a jerk of his head. 'I fell right down, I think I've sprained my ankle.'

'It looks more than a sprain to me!' in her smart work costume, she crouched down to examine his foot, carefully extending her gentle fingers to touch the misshapen ankle. 'You've broken it, Jeremy. I'll call the ambulance.'

'No, no, I don't want a fuss. It's just a sprain, it'll get easier soon. It just needs a strong bandage, a wet one, bound very tight . . .'

'Look, this is more than a sprain, see the way it's bent? You need the hospital. I'll call the ambulance.'

'No, love, no, I don't want all that fuss and blue lights flashing, horns blaring and so on. You could run me in . . . or if you're going to work, George next door might do it . . . it's only five minutes into Ashfordly General, I can be there before the ambulance gets here. They'll check me over and bandage me up, then I can come home . . . no problem.'

'I'll run you in then, I'll ring and tell them at work I'll be late.'

'I thought you had an important meeting of some kind this morning? You've got your best costume on.'

'You're more important than a boring old meeting . . .'

'No, love, no. You can't miss the meeting because of a mere sprain! Pop round to see if George can do it, he's retired, he's got nothing else to do and he owes me a favour for fixing that broken window in his garage. I'm not at death's door. You must go to work! Me and George can cope.'

'Well, if you insist . . .'

'I do.'

And so it was that George Newton from next door found himself helping Jeremy into his car with the aid of a broom as a crutch; there was a good deal of pained shouting and cursing but it wasn't long before Jeremy was safely aboard in as comfortable a position as he could find, and being chauffeured into Ashfordly General Hospital.

Elizabeth said she would ring the hospital from the office to learn the extent of his injuries but Jeremy was adamant it was nothing more than a bad sprain which could be dealt with very speedily; in fact, she would ring the hospital now to warn the Casualty Department that her husband was on his way with a suspected broken ankle.

It was shortly after George and Jeremy had left Aidensfield that I became involved in this modest domestic drama. George Newton, a retired accountant in his 70s, was perhaps not the best of drivers particularly in a stressful and urgent situation and he was hurrying perhaps too much along the lanes between Aidensfield and Ashfordly. When he reached the junction at Briggsby, where the minor road enters the main road at a busy junction, he shot straight out instead of pausing to gauge the speed of oncoming vehicles. An articulated lorry happened to be approaching from the left and although its driver did his best to avoid the fool who failed to slow down at the junction, his vehicle rammed the side of George's Vauxhall and sent it spinning on to the verge where it came to rest on its side in a convenient hedgerow.

The two men in the Vauxhall were trapped because the body of the car had crumpled under the impact but the lorry driver was not injured; he spotted the telephone kiosk near the junction, rang the emergency services and soon the ambulance, fire brigade and police were racing to the scene, the task of the fire brigade being to release the two injured men.

There is no need to detail the action I had to take at the scene, other than to say I had to take relevant measurements, obtain statements from witnesses, make sure no further accidents resulted and eventually submit my Road Traffic Accident Report.

No one was killed; the lorry driver, although shocked, suffered no physical injuries, George Newton had a broken left arm, a cracked skull and cheekbone, and lots of cuts and bruises. In addition to his broken left ankle, Jeremy Flanders broke his right leg, thus he finished up in hospital with two broken legs.

I went to visit him in his hospital bed when he was fit enough to provide me with a statement; he smiled and said, 'You know, Mr Rhea, I could have been killed. I was very lucky, wasn't I?'

Chapter 4

There were two mainstream churches in Aidensfield, the Catholic church of St Aidan after whom the village was named, and the Anglican church of All Saints. There was also a Russian Orthodox church based in a caravan with an onion shaped golden coloured structure on its roof and a former Methodist chapel which has since been converted into a small dwelling house.

The Catholic church was fairly modern, having been built in the late 1950s on the site of a Norman church which had borne the name of St Aidan but which had been destroyed during the Reformation. The Anglican church, although looking quite ancient with its squat tower and rugged stone construction, dated to Victorian times and replaced a smaller post-Reformation building which had stood on the same site. Both mainstream churches were well patronized with active congregations but each had a problem. Their graveyards were always a mess, although neither the Russian Orthodox nor the Methodists had their own graveyard. If required they made use respectively of the Catholic and Anglican burial grounds.

Apart from the most recent graves, all the others were

permanently overgrown with briars, grass and weeds while on regular occasions litter was blown into the churchyard or even dropped there by visitors. The older graves were neglected, tombstones tended to lean at awkward angles and in some cases artificial flowers remained in containers having been there for years because no one had thought to remove them or replace them with real flowers. Some tombstones were covered with moss which made their inscriptions illegible.

In short, both churchyards were usually a mess. Both Father Simon of St Aidan's and the Reverend Lord of All Saints made repeated attempts to find willing volunteers to maintain the graveyards but even when such efforts were successful, the volunteers rarely stuck to their resolve for more than a few weeks. The snag with using volunteers was that they could not be ordered to work – they had to be asked nicely and they had to accommodate this extra work within their own busy domestic schedules. Another worry was that some would quickly become disillusioned by the scale of the effort required to please both the church authorities and relatives of the deceased. Some relatives, usually the worst in neglecting the final resting places of their loved ones, made the loudest complaints of official neglect. More often than not, the volunteers gave up their work within a few weeks and in such a small community, it was difficult finding yet another willing helper. To add to the woes, neither church had the funds to pay for the necessary regular upkeep.

Finding someone to care for the churchyards and graves on a regular basis was one of those problems which never went away and which was never entirely resolved. Placing sheep in the churchyards to mow the grass had once been tried with limited success because they tended to eat any freshly-placed grave flowers as well as the grass – and so the graves were usually rather bare. It was planned that the sheep would be introduced from time to time to do their grass-cutting, hopefully when there were no new graves bearing fresh flowers but it could be guaranteed that once the sheep were installed, however temporarily, someone would turn up to place flowers on a grave. The sheep munched them in no time at all.

Alternatively, a resident would die the minute the sheep were introduced which meant fresh flowers would appear and so the sheep found themselves banned yet again. In addition, some thought that having sheep roaming among the graves was an insult to the dignity of the deceased. A permanent satisfactory answer to the solution seemed therefore to elude the clergymen, their respective parish councils and their congregations.

Quite unexpectedly, however, a letter arrived simultaneously at both the Catholic and Anglican churches. From Canada, the correspondence was identical in both cases and was signed by a lady called Monica Stowell. She explained she was researching her family history and had discovered an Amos Stowell who lived in Aidensfield during the early years of the nineteenth century. It seemed that fairly recent generations of Stowells had also lived in the village, even into the post World War II period. She was anxious to trace anyone of that name, or anyone who had married someone of that name, and then said she would be travelling from Canada in about two months time to make a search of the churchyards for any Stowell graves. She also expressed the hope she might be allowed to examine parish registers for any records of weddings, births or deaths of any Stowells or their relatives. Then came the important piece of news – she wanted to donate money to whichever church or churches contained her deceased relatives' graves so that they could be tended, weeded and carefully maintained now and for the foreseeable future. As a gesture of goodwill, she would pay for the immediate tidying of the entire churchyard or yards in question – she knew how such places soon became overgrown and neglected.

She offered £150 for the immediate work and said that whatever was not used could be placed in a fund she would establish to maintain the entire churchyard or churchyards in perpetuity. She thought that some of her forebears were Catholic and some were Protestant, hence her approach to both churches.

The arrival of her letter prompted a most surprising reaction. Father Simon and the Reverend Christian Lord decided to have a meeting to discuss the possibility of a joint operation to maintain their churchyards. The notion of finding someone to tend both had never previously been discussed – hitherto, each had operated quite independently of the other. Now, it seemed, they could work together on a joint mission because a lady from overseas had offered a sum of money for the care of her long-deceased family grave or graves wherever they were. Both agreed that work should begin immediately so that the churchyards, and especially any Stowell graves that might be discovered, should be in pristine condition by the time of her arrival. The work involved was not merely cutting grass and removing dead flowers – it entailed maintenance of gravestones even to the extent of removing mossy growths and highlighting any faded lettering or inscriptions, it would mean renovating the surrounds of some graves and perhaps renewing the gravel walking areas around the more expensive or elaborate ones, it might mean replacing containers for flowers or replanting bulbs . . . and the money promised was sufficient for a thoroughly professional job to be undertaken without delay and maintained over a considerable period.

This then raised the question of who had the time and skill to fulfil such a task; it was not a job for an unreliable volunteer nor was it something which could be achieved with only a scythe, hoe and rake. A professional had to be found, someone with multi-skills and the equipment necessary to perform all the tasks.

'Any suggestions, Nick?' asked Father Simon when he told me about this development one Sunday after Mass. 'I've looked at my congregation and there's no one among them who could do it, and Christian Lord has done the same. He's got no one to ask, we don't want volunteers for this.'

'Then you'll have to look outside both congregations,' I smiled. 'There are lots of people who don't go to any church even in Aidensfield and among them, I'm sure there'll be someone who'll be keen to earn good money for doing that work.'

'We priests tend to forget that there are people who don't go to church on Sunday!' he laughed. 'We do get a little unworldly, I suppose, very inward looking. So you get around a lot, Nick, can you suggest anyone?'

'How about Claude Jeremiah Greengrass?'

'Now there's an idea! I never thought of him, he rarely, if ever, sets foot inside a church unless he's attending a funeral. You think he could cope? And, more important, can he do a good job?'

'You'd have to keep a close eye on him but he could do it, he's certainly very capable even if he is sometimes a bit devious. He's been tending gardens around here for years, cutting lawns and hedges, making paths, weeding, picking potatoes, even re-building walls and laying paths. And he's got all the necessary equipment to do a proper job. He'd never volunteer to do it free of charge but if he smells money, he'll do it. I think, though, it might be an idea if you and Christian Lord get together to arrange for him to be supervised by members of your parish councils. Make sure he knows it's a case of: no proper work, no pay! And make sure you pay him when he's finished, not before he starts! Otherwise he'll never start. And don't tell him how much money has been offered, he'll want the lot. Keep him on tenterhooks, that's the sort of supervision he needs! It's the proverbial carrot being dangled before the donkey!'

And so it was that Claude Jeremiah Greengrass was invited to a meeting at the Vicarage, not really knowing what lay in store for him and wondering why on earth two men of the cloth would wish to discuss anything with him. The vicar, quite skilled in getting the best out of people, made sure Claude was well looked after during the meeting, being offered coffee and biscuits by Ruth Lord, and even a glass of sherry, then he was taken on a tour of the Anglican churchyard, following by a similar visit to the Catholic one after which the proposal was put to him. Both clergymen, doubtless having been briefed by their councils, were careful not to mention money at the outset and the result was that Claude listened to their pleas, and then said, 'No, no, I can't take this on. I'm not a churchgoer anyway, and as for taking on two churchyards which have been neglected for years, well, I mean, you can surely find someone from your flocks, can't you? Sheep even,' and he laughed at his own joke.

'We're looking for a professional, Mr Greengrass,' said Christian Lord. 'If you can't accept our offer perhaps you could recommend someone? We will pay good fees, of course, for the right person.'

'Pay? Did I hear you say pay?'

'Yes, didn't we mention that? We wouldn't expect this kind of major undertaking to be done for nothing. We have a lady benefactor called Monica Stowell who is coming from Canada in a couple of months or so, seeking her ancestors, and we need to have the graveyards in peak condition when she arrives. She will pay for this work and so one of the tasks will be to seek out any tombstones bearing that surname and make sure they are renovated in time for her arrival. Clean the lettering, straighten up the stones, put gravel down where necessary, flowers near the time of her arrival and so on. Meanwhile, Father Simon and I will be scouring the parish records for any Stowells and anyone they might have married. It's a big job, Mr Greengrass, and an important one, so we need the best possible operator. If we make a good job of this, she might consider a permanent income for maintaining those graves . . . if you get my drift!'

'Aye, I see what you mean even if I've never heard that name hereabouts,' and Claude blinked rapidly at the thought of earning useful and regular sums of money, especially in the village where he wouldn't have to travel far to work, and so he asked, 'So, I mean, if I decide I might just be able to fit you in, being a very busy sort of chap whose skills are in great demand all over the place, how much would it be worth to me?'

'I think you should provide us with your hourly rate, Mr Greengrass, and then you can have another look at both churchyards to estimate how long you expect the work would take, in the first instance to make a good job of tidying both churchyards, renovating the gravestones and so forth. A simple multiplication sum will provide us with an idea of the sort of fee you'd expect for that first phase.'

'Aye, well, I can do that.'

'Remember we're talking of a substantial contract here, Mr Greengrass, it's not just a few week's work. If the initial project turns out satisfactorily, there may be more commissions in the future, but of course once the main hard work is done, continuing maintance will not be quite so demanding, time-consuming or expensive. This is a wonderful opportunity for us both and I am sure you will ensure things work out to our mutual satisfaction.'

'Aye, well, there'll allus be a demand for good clean churchyards and well tended graves, folks are allus grumbling about the state of them but generally folks never have time to care for 'em. Right, well, let me think about this after I've done a recce of both churchyards.'

The Revd. Lord reminded Claude that Monica Stowell was expected at Aidensfield in a couple of month's time and so his first phase must be properly completed prior to her arrival and it must be done to the satisfaction of both churches. Claude said he would not fail and beamed in anticipation of a regular income, then went off to do his sums. He returned the following day to announce he would renovate both churchyards within two months at a total cost of £100.

Included in that charge would be a daily check on their condition, such as discarded litter and dead flowers, until the arrival of the lady in question. With £50 to spare, therefore, money of which Claude was unaware, he was asked to complete the work. He accepted, his only stipulation being that he was paid in cash. Both churchmen agreed, and said, 'Yes, on completion.'

And so it was that Claude set about his mammoth task of tidying two severely neglected churchyards and there is no doubt he produced a huge improvement. First he cleared away all the surplus undergrowth, briars and nettles, then he removed the accumulated rubbish, cut the grass, weeded paths and got rid of ancient flower containers. Both the clergymen and members of their parish councils paid periodic visits and all expressed great satisfaction as Claude set about cleaning and stabilising the older tombstones, using a stonemason's chisel to remove moss from some lettering and re-whitening other letters with a small pot of paint.

He was hard at work one Wednesday afternoon when I popped into St Aidan's to have a chat with Father Simon. A confidence trickster was operating in the north of England, preying on Catholic priests by saying he'd spent time in a priest's training college but had left due to a crisis of faith, and was now trying to 'find' himself as he toured the country seeking some kind of worthwhile occupation. He asked for financial help and some priests had believed his story, giving him various amounts from £5 to £25. His story was a complete fabrication and so I had to warn all my local Catholic priests. Which I did.

When I left, I spotted Claude working on the lettering of a gravestone and shouted a greeting across to him. 'Well done, Claude. Keep up the good work! You'll get your reward in heaven!'

'I'm not concerned with heavenly rewards, constable, I

think in terms of earthly rewards for a job done well, usually in the shape of pound notes. I'll tell you what, though, I haven't found any of those Stowell graves yet, not here nor across the road in the Anglican place.'

'Really? Maybe they're very old and well hidden.'

'Well, I'm working backwards in both places, doing the more modern ones first because they happen to be easiest to get at, so I might come across a Stowell grave before too long, tucked out of sight somewhere among the rubbish at the back.'

As the days passed, I chatted to Father Simon and Christian Lord, usually about Claude's excellent progress. Although he was not working full time in the churchyards, he did spend a lot of his working day there and evidence of his impact was plain to see. Both were almost in pristine condition and there is no doubt it was due to Claude's hard work. I was reminded of his claim that he'd not yet found a Stowell grave when Christian Lord said the same thing during one of our informal chats. He'd not found any Stowell grave nor had he found any reference to the name in his parish records. And neither had Father Simon. Both thought the reason was that the local Stowells had perhaps married into other families and in fact, Father Simon suggested they should write to Monica before she set off for England, explaining that they had so far failed to find any trace of her ancestors.

The two priests therefore wrote a joint letter to explain this lack of news, but nonetheless allowed Claude to continue his work while they pored over yet more ancient records. By then, of course, he was on the last lap and was performing a maintenance task rather than heavy clearance – still with no sign of any Stowell grave. However, it appears that their letters crossed in the trans-Atlantic post because a couple of days after posting their letter, the priests received one from Monica which announced her date of arrival. Just one week from that day. A Wednesday.

Claude was given this news so that he could ensure the graves and churchyards were in the peak of condition, thanks to her generosity; they would prove her money had been well spent. And so, in those final days, the clergymen, the parish councils and even the congregation, plus members of some families still living in the area even if they were non-churchgoers, all went to admire their wonderful new places of eternal peace and contentment. It is fair to say that both churchyards had been transformed into wonderful examples of how such places should be maintained and cared for.

And then came the bombshell. Father Simon received a telephone call from Monica to say she had just received the letter about the non-discovery of any Stowell graves or names in Aidensfield. That had caused her to have another closer look at her own records whereupon she had realized the village should have been Ardensfleet which she thought was somewhere on the coast of Norfolk. She had made the mistake due to misreading the village name – some ancestor's handwriting in her records was not very clear, she admitted.

She apologized for the mistake and thanked them for their efforts but made no reference to the money she had promised. It meant, of course, that now there were no funds to pay Claude. It was clear there would have to be a meeting to discuss the dilemma but now it would involve both clergymen as well as their respective parish councils. Even before the meeting, word of this reached my ears with some people saying Monica should be asked to honour her original promise and pay Claude, and others saying the churches should share the cost between them even if it meant digging deep into some reserve funds, while yet another faction felt Claude should not be paid anything on the grounds that others had done similar work voluntarily in the past. Due to other commitments, the meeting was planned for a week the following Monday.

It was inevitable that Claude should discover this impasse. When the expected date of Monica's arrival came without any sign of her and without any sign of any payment, Claude smelt the proverbial rat and was soon knocking on the door of the Vicarage, demanding to see the Reverend Lord. I was not present of course, but was told by the vicar that Claude had not said a word before presenting a piece of paper. It was a bill.

'A hundred pounds I am owed,' he had said to the vicar. 'I don't know where that woman has got to, I don't know why she hasn't turned up and I don't know why we've not found her ancestors' graves but I do know I have honoured my part of the bargain, I do know I have done a good job in those graveyards and I do know I am owed the money I was promised. No pay, no more work, vicar!'

'Monica mistook our village for another, Claude, but she hasn't mentioned any money and won't be coming. I'll make sure you get a cheque.'

'Cash, vicar, the deal was for cash. No cheques. I've worked my socks off on this project so I don't want to be put off by weak excuses. I'll be back tomorrow when I'll expect £100 in notes.'

And he stomped away, his disgust evident for all to see.

Christian Lord and Father Simon arranged a hurried meeting and their charitable sense overcame their business sense because they decided Claude must be paid, in cash as promised, and that each church would have to bear fifty per cent of his fee. In the absence of both church treasurers, each managed to find £50 in cash before Claude returned, but then had the task of persuading their respective councils to somehow replace the money which each had paid of their private and personal funds. It had been an expensive exercise for both men.

I was not privy to any discussions which followed but I do know that Claude never offered again to keep the churchyards tidy, either voluntarily or for a fee.

Another of Claude's mishaps occurred when he spoke to a local nosey-parker without really thinking about what he was saying. The famously nosey person was Mrs Freda Hammond who lived in Elsinby. She was a widow aged about fifty, her late husband having worked in the planning department of Ashfordly Rural District Council.

A large heavy lady, she was surprisingly active because she walked for miles every day. Living alone in the village, she hated being confined to her tidy little cottage and spent most of her time tramping around the village or even going for longer walks into the neighbouring communities. Wherever she went, however, she would exercise her annoying inquisitiveness. With her considerable frame, mass of grey hair, round red face, thick brown overcoat and heavy walking shoes, she was a familiar sight in and around Elsinby. In addition, she could often be seen walking along the road to Aidensfield, or the lane which led to Ploatby and even outwards along the York road towards Craydale. And during her rambles, there was more than enough to excite her interest.

Although she was otherwise a pleasant woman with a very kind and considerate nature, her inquisitiveness made her less than welcome. If she was walking past a garden, for example, she would peer over the hedge to see how well it was maintained and if anyone was working there, she would ask, 'What are you doing? Are those carrots you're planting? When did you last cut that lawn?' Or if a woman was hanging out her washing, she might say, 'Is that your week's washing or just a few days? Those pillow cases aren't very white, are they? My mother always washed on a Monday, you know, and wouldn't have any truck with these new fangled washing machines, they leave the whites grey, she always said.' Even in the shop or post office, she would ask of another customer, 'What are you buying today? You really must like those fruit cakes, buying as many as you do,' or 'Who are you writing to this week? You must spend a fortune on stamps.'

Similarly, she might ask the butcher, 'Will you be calling on Mrs Brown today? I suppose she'll be getting her usual sausages and liver,' or 'I'll bet that Mrs Jessop who's just moved in to number twelve would like some of your best steak, she seems to have plenty of money to spend.' If she saw a family packing their car for a day's outing, she would ask, 'So where are you going today? Scarborough again, is it? Or the zoo this time? That must be expensive for a family like yours,' and she might say to a villager, 'Was that your mother you had staying with you last weekend? I saw her bedroom curtains were closed until about eleven, wasn't she very well? I saw her buying that bottle of sherry in the off-licence in Ashfordly.' One day she accosted me as I was going to visit an Aidensfield gentleman to obtain a statement from him; he'd witnessed a road traffic accident in

Whitby and I had to ask him to provide an account of the event. When Mrs Hammond saw me opening his garden gate, she said, 'Are you going to see Mr Youngman? I'll bet that son of his has got himself into bother again, he never was very reliable, you know. And what about that wife of his? She got another pair of new shoes last week . . . really, I don't know how she does it.'

Her undisguised inquisitiveness mean that if anyone saw her approaching, they would do their best to avoid her but she was usually a match for anyone who tried to evade her questions. But it was Claude who succeeded in a rather spectacular manner. It happened like this.

In their wisdom, the parish councillors of Ploatby, a tiny hamlet along the lane from Elsinby, decided the village green required some kind of focal point.

As things were, there was merely a patch of grass in the centre with nothing else – no war memorial, no horse trough, no market cross, no ancient lock-up, no stocks or whipping post, no pond, nothing. In fact, as they stressed at their meeting, there was nothing to attract visitors or tourists, nothing to persuade travellers to halt awhile to enjoy Ploatby's undoubted charms. If the tourists now flocking to other parts of the dale could be persuaded to halt awhile in Ploatby, it might generate something like a tea shop which would serve the village and even provide some modest employment.

After much deliberation it was decided that something suitably rustic should be placed on the small green and when Councillor Collins suggested a parish pump, everyone thought it was a marvellous idea. Because there was no water supply on the green however, and to prevent children messing about with the pump, it was decided that a mock but realistic-looking pump would be ideal. It would look the part without presenting too many problems. And, as Councillor Collins pointed out, he knew where a beautiful specimen could be obtained – he'd seen it among other junk on Claude Jeremiah Greengrass's ramshackle ranch. It was a genuine pump which had been removed from some other village in the past and it could be established on Ploatby Green minus a water supply, and thus provide a traditional and instantly recognizable rustic focal point. He felt sure the cost would not be prohibitive – not many people wanted defunct parish pumps of doubtful vintage. The other councillors thought it was a grand idea, and they even decided Claude Jeremiah should be the man to site it in the appropriate place on a new concrete base.

The pump could be renovated and painted in a handsome dark green colour. And so the deal was done. Claude sold the pump for a modest profit and accepted the commission to install it. It provided a nice little job for him while getting rid of a large lump of surplus scrap metal: It was a couple of weeks later as he was digging out the foundations that Mrs Hammond passed during one of her excursions. She had briskly walked along the lane from Elsinby and was inhaling the fresh country air when she spotted Claude at work and came across to see what he was doing.

'Ah, Mr Greengrass! What's that you're building?'

Claude, knowing of her desperate inquisitiveness while being rather keen to teach her a lesson, replied, 'Aye, well, it's the new public toilets, you know. It's a National Park initiative. To cope with visitors. I'm preparing the base.'

'New toilets? In Ploatby?'

'They'll be very smart, Mrs Hammond, it's a most fashionable design with state of the art plumbing. Hot and cold water on tap. Mirrors. You name it, these toilets will have it all. Just what the tourists need and it'll just cost a penny a go.'

'Then you tell me this, Mr Greengrass, if Ploatby can have new toilets, why can't Elsinby? Just you answer me that. I have been campaigning for years to have public toilets in Elsinby, it's a busy village on a main road with visitors stopping to look at the stream, visit the church and walk up to the castle, and there's no public toilets. Now what has Ploatby got? No church, no castle, no stream, no pub, nothing. And it's off the beaten track, nobody will find their way here. So why can Ploatby have toilets when Elsinby can't? Just you answer me that, Mr Greengrass.'

'Search me!' and he spread his hands in a gesture of hopelessness. 'I'm just the chap who's got the job of installing them. I just do as I'm told.'

'Well, I'm going to see about this!' she snapped. 'I shall demand to know why Ploatby has been allowed toilets while Elsinby can't have them. It's all wrong, Mr Greengrass, all completely wrong. Leave this with me . . . my dear husband worked in the planning department, so I know how to get answers out of the council, mark my words!' And she stomped off back to Elsinby as Claude smiled in quiet success.

The first thing Mrs Hammond did was to ring the *Ashfordly Gazette* to demand they published a piece about the injustice but, as good reporters do, a representative of the paper rang Ashfordly Council to check the story. He was told there were no plans to build toilets in either Elsinby or Ploatby which, of course, made the reporter highly suspicious that something underhand was probably going on. In the minds of some journalists, an official denial is usually an indication of a cover-up so when a photographer went to Ploatby that evening, after Claude had gone home and when no one else was abroad in the village, to find the foundations of a new structure already being prepared, it reinforced his suspicions. He took a photograph of the mysterious new hole whereupon the paper felt it had enough evidence to publish an article about the affair. It was titled 'The Great Ploatby Toilet Mystery' with quotes from Mrs Hammond to say how disgusted she was that tiny, off-the-beaten-track Ploatby could have public toilets when the larger, busier tourist-trail Elsinby had been refused those facilities, not once but several times over the years.

A quote from the Ashfordly Rural District Council denied that Ploatby had been given permission to install public toilets and added that no one from the hamlet had applied for planning permission – and that merely added more fuel to the proverbial flames. If toilets were being erected in Ploatby, then they would surely be in breach of planning regulations.

When I was patrolling those villages on the day the story broke in the Gazette, I popped into the Hopbind Inn at Elsinby in the course of my duty and found it full of angry villagers who even went to far as to suggest that Ploatby residents should be banned from drinking there. The general feeling was that it was utterly wrong that such a tiny community should have a public toilet when a busy, thriving metropolis like Elsinby was denied one. I had to admit a total lack of knowledge of Ploatby's proposed toilets but, out of curiosity and wishing to enhance my local knowledge, I drove along the lane to Ploatby. And there I found Claude Jeremiah Greengass hard at work, clearly constructing the foundations for some new structure. A concrete mixer was noisily rotating nearby and he had a pile of hard-core near the large hole he had dug.

'Now then, Claude,' I parked and went across to see what he was doing.

'Whatever it is, Constable, I didn't do it,' he grinned.

'So this is the site of the new toilet block, is it?' I said. 'It looks mighty small to me.'

'She's spread the news, has she? That Hammond woman?'

'It's all over the *Gazette* this morning,' I said. 'The people of Elsinby are hopping mad, they're talking of banning Ploatby folk from the pub, so you can see how serious it is. Elsinby think they should be given toilets before Ploatby.'

'Aye, well, I must say I would agree with that, being a regular at the Hopbind but this isn't a toilet block, you know.'

'I thought it looked a bit small! So what is it?'

'A parish pump, well, a replica, it's in the back of my truck,' and he told me all about the new focal point.

'So why did Mrs Hammond think this was a new toilet block?' I asked.

'Because I told the nosey old devil that's what it was, to teach her a lesson, to make her keep her nose out of things.'

'Well, she's certainly caused a rumpus,' I laughed. 'She's got two villages at loggerheads, a false report in the *Gazette*, and the council doing its best to deny something that isn't happening anyway!'

I have no idea how Mrs Hammond coped with the fact she had been wonderfully misled by Claude but I did hear she had walked along the lane to Ploatby to see what he was really constructing. When he said it was a fake parish pump, she smiled and nodded, 'Well, at least I got those toilets stopped, Mr Greengrass!'

'But you haven't got a parish pump in Elsinby!' he retorted.

'No, but we do have a castle and a church and a pub.'

'Then mebbe a public toilet block is a good idea,' he said.

'The council is considering the matter,' she beamed. 'You see, Mr Greengrass, I do know how to get things done.'

Chapter 5

It was shortly after 10 a.m. on a Tuesday morning in June and I was in the office attached to my police house on the hill top at Aidensfield when someone knocked on the door. At the beginning of each tour of duty, I spent an hour in my office, partially to catch up with administrative matters and partially to be available if anyone wanted to contact me upon routine, non-urgent matters. It was, I suppose, rather like a surgery and on that particular day I was due to work a day shift – 9 a.m. to 5 p.m. A shift with those hours was always considered a luxury, far better than working through the night or at the crack of dawn! It meant I could have the warm and light summer evening at home – unless something unexpected happened to compel me to return to duty.

By ten, I had completed my paperwork and was about to embark on a tour of duty in my minivan when I heard that knock. I opened the door to find a couple of middle aged people standing there, a man and a woman, both dressed in hiking gear and each bearing a large rucksack, hanging from the bottom of which was a small single tent with its accompanying poles.

'Come in,' I invited.

My office was like a miniature police station because it had a wooden counter and was filled with my filing cabinets, desk, typewriter, wall hooks bearing uniform, important posters and notices and all the other paraphernalia befitting a rural constable. But without cells! When I opened the door to them, I was dressed in my uniform but without a tunic or cap.

I was wearing my blue shirt with long sleeves and perhaps I might have looked like a postman or railway porter.

'You are the policeman?' the man asked politely.

'PC Rhea,' I introduced myself. 'The village policeman here in Aidensfield.'

'John and Rosie Marshall,' he responded. 'From Manchester, we're on a walking and camping holiday on the moors. Er, we're not quite sure whether we should report this, it might be some sort of joke but there again it might not . . .'

'It sounds interesting, whatever it is!' I smiled. 'Obviously, you've decided it should be reported.'

'Yes,' Mr Marshall acted as spokesman for the couple. 'Er, well, Mr Rhea, we've found a coffin. On the moors.'

'A coffin? An old one? Has it been exposed by erosion? From one of those howes up there?'

'No, it's a brand new one, light oak I think, with chrome handles. Very modern and in excellent condition, it's not an ancient one by any means.'

'Really? So you can guess my next question,' I didn't know whether to laugh at this or treat it seriously. 'Is it full or empty?'

'I don't know, we didn't look, it's got a lid on, by the way, screwed down.'

'Does it have a name on?' I was rapidly trying to remember the sort of things one might expect to find on a coffin, such as a plate bearing the name of the deceased or even the undertaker's name.

'Nothing,' he said. 'It's just a smart new-looking coffin.'

'Could it have fallen from the back of a hearse?' I pondered aloud.

'Not where we found it, Mr Rhea,' said Mr Marshall in all seriousness. 'It's well off any beaten track, it's in a very remote part of the moors, almost hidden under some bracken. We just happened to see it as we were walking down the ghyll.'

'Can you show me where it is?'

He pulled a crumpled Ordnance Survey map from a pocket in his trousers leg and spread it across my counter. Then he pointed to a place called Goverdale Ghyll, ghyll being the name for a tumbling moorland stream. It was about a mile from Shelvingby in a tiny dale; I knew the point where the ghyll entered the river at Shelvingby. It was on my beat.

'It's on the lower half of that ghyll,' he said. 'Ten minutes or so walk from the village. About there,' and he prodded a location with his finger. 'We're camping, by the way, so we had an early start this morning. We found it just after seven, then walked through Shelvingby until we found a bus which brought us here. We're heading for the coast, taking things day by day although we might stop at a bed-and-breakfast if we need a bath!'

'Do you think I can find the coffin without you showing me the way? I don't want to disrupt your holiday unnecessarily.'

'Well, there's a public footpath up the side of Goverdale Ghyll, and the coffin will be on your left as you climb, as I said, only about ten minutes walk from the village at the bottom. Just where I showed you.'

'Right, well, I'll go and have a look for it. Now, you won't have a fixed address on this holiday, will you? Or anywhere I can contact you?'

'No, we've no idea where we'll be spending the nights, and we're away for another week or so, but I can give you our home address, or I could ring you later from a kiosk to find out what's happened.'

And so I obtained their home address and provided them with my telephone number, then jokingly said, 'I'll record this as found property. If we have no reports of it being lost and it's not claimed within three months, it becomes yours!'

'I don't want a coffin!' he sounded alarmed. 'Well, not yet anyway! Not while I'm alive and kicking.'

'Hang on a second,' I said. 'Before you go, I'll ring our local police station to see if it's been reported stolen or lost.'

I rang Ashfordly Police Station and PC Alf Ventress answered.

'It's Nick here at Aidensfield, Alf. Have we any reports of a coffin being lost or stolen? A new one in light oak with chrome handles. I've a report of one being found and am about to go and investigate it but thought I'd better check first.'

'I can't say we've had many reports of lost or stolen coffins, Nick, there's not really a criminal demand for stolen coffins or second-hand ones for that matter, but I'll check just in case someone reported it missing before I came on duty.'

He checked his records but there was no report and so I allowed the Marshalls to continue their walking holiday as I set out to investigate their report.

I hoped it wasn't a hoax really, I should have asked them to escort me to its whereabouts but I couldn't have fitted both into my van to transport them there unless one sat on the floor in the rear. I did not think that was very dignified and in any case felt sure their report was genuine. After a coffee, I started my van, radioed Control to report going on air and set off to Shelvingby on my unusual quest. It was a drive of about twenty five minutes and when I arrived, I parked near the church, put on my hiking boots, placed a selection of screwdrivers in my pocket from the van's tool kit and set off to climb Goverdale Ghyll.

It was a steep, rocky and testing route beside the tumbling water, not the sort of exercise one would choose on a hot June day while clad in a policeman's uniform but eventually, after some ten minutes of hard climbing I found the coffin. It had been pushed deep into the cover of tall bracken and only one end – the foot end – was visible. Even then, I thought most passers-by would not notice it – in my case, of course, I was specifically seeking it. It was just as Mr Marshall had described – a neat clean and very new-looking coffin in what looked like light oak with chrome handles. It was very clean too; obviously, it hadn't been here very long. My next task was to check its contents. It did not take many moments to loosen the screws which held down the lid and when I removed it, I was relieved to find it empty. From what I could see, it looked as if it had never been used – it was in pristine condition both inside and out but with no kind of inner lining. I replaced the lid and screwed it down. Now what should I do? Leave it here in case someone came to collect it? Or take it away with me and enter it into our 'Found Property' ledger?

I didn't think the sergeant would be very pleased to find

a coffin in his Found Property cupboard but I thought the local paper might make a feature out of the story. The right kind of publicity might result in the loser coming forward or, failing that, produce some explanation for its presence on that moorland hillside. I decided to leave it, at least for the time being. I could always return later to see whether it had been removed although if I needed to retrieve it, I might need help in carrying it to my van. I had no idea of the weight of an empty wooden coffin, but its shape and size alone would make it cumbersome and not at all easy for one person to carry, especially down a steep hillside along a rock-strewn path.

I pondered the notion that, had there been snow on the ground, I could have sat inside it and used it as a toboggan, a wonderful and rather exciting means of getting both it and myself back down to the village. And so I left it where it was.

Back in Shelvingby with my police boots having replaced my hiking footwear I decided to ask a few of the residents if they could offer any explanation for this mystery. Someone or something might have been noticed by an alert person but Shelvingby is a very small community with a single shop which also contains the post office. Apart from a very smart inn and an isolated Methodist chapel, it has about fifty or sixty residents and a few farms scattered around the outskirts on the moor, although in summer it is usually busy with hikers passing through and tourists coming by car to explore the neighbouring landscape. Not exactly a thriving Metropolis. The shop was my first calling place because it overlooked the route from the ghyll.

Anyone walking up or down past the site of the coffin would either emerge into or leave Shelvingby at that point.

The shopkeeper was called Mrs Hollins.

'Hello, PC Rhea,' she beamed when I walked into the tiny room crammed with every conceivable domestic requirement. 'It's not often we see you in these parts.'

'That's because you're such a law-abiding community!' I gave the expected answer. 'I'm not needed here, you're all so well-behaved.'

'I'm not so sure about some of those tourists,' she said. 'They're not averse to stealing stones from our garden walls to put on their rockeries back in town, or nicking flowers from our gardens instead of buying them in shops. We don't leave anything useful lying about in our gardens during the tourist season. You'd be surprised how many spades and hoes go missing. Maybe we should report the thefts?'

'That would play havoc with our crime statistics! All those undetected crimes – the answer is to lock things away. But yes, we should be made aware of all crimes.'

'I think we all know that, it's just carelessness on our part. Anyway, what brings you here today?'

'A coffin,' I said. 'Do you know anyone who might have lost or mislaid one?'

'A coffin? A real one?'

'Very real, very new, very smart,' I said. 'In perfect condition, ready for use. Very low mileage and one very careful owner, I'd say. And it's empty, I should add. It's up on the moor near Goverdale Ghyll – how it got there and why it's there is what I'm trying to find out. And I've no idea how long it's been there although it doesn't look weathered. I'd say it arrived very recently.'

'Well, I can't help you with that, Mr Rhea, we've no undertaker in this village as you know, the local folks use Harold Poulter from Ashfordly or Bernie Scripps from

Aidensfield. I can't think why an empty coffin should suddenly appear on our moors and I've no idea where it's come from.'

'Well, perhaps you'd discuss it with your customers, see if the villagers can throw any light on the affair. I'll pop up to the hotel and see if anyone there can help.'

The Laverock Hotel stood high and proud overlooking Shelvingby and it was popular with visitors. Although it was more of an hotel than a rural inn, it did have a bar which was well patronized by the locals while a high proportion of its everchanging residents were fishermen, grouse shooting men from home and overseas or followers of foxhunts who came for some part of each season. I popped into the bar; my uniform and the fact I was on duty meaning I could not take a drink. The barman was called Eric; he was on duty when I arrived, preparing for the lunchtime influx of customers but the bar was empty.

'Hello, Mr Rhea, a bit early for checking us, isn't it? You usually turn up at closing time, not opening time!'

'I've got a puzzle, Eric,' and I told him about the coffin.

'The only strangers I've seen, who were not our customers, were a couple of lads who came in late last night, not long before closing time, asking if they could use the phone. They were hikers with all the gear, boots, rucksacks, the lot. One looked very poorly, I thought, and his mate wanted to get him to a doctor.'

'Local, were they?'

'No, I'd never seen them before. They said they'd been doing the Lyke Wake Walk and he'd been taken ill, stomach trouble he said, so because we've no doctor in the village I showed him where the phone was and he rang for a taxi.'

'They were doing the Lyke Wake Walk, you say?'

'That's what they said.'

I knew the route of the Lyke Wake Walk passed across the moors above Shelvingby, but its nearest point would be at least two miles away. Certainly, the route did not pass through Shelvingby village and if one of those walkers had been taken ill high on those moors, then it was quite feasible they would head for Shelvingby – the nearest village – to seek help. There was another clue there too, and that is what interested me because it provided just a flicker of understanding as to why that coffin might be lying on the moor.

The Lyke Wake Walk is a long distance trek across the highest and widest part of the North York Moors, the route stretching from Scarth Nick between Swainby and Osmotherley on the western edge of the moors to Wyke Point near Ravenscar on the east coast. Its founder, Bill Cowley, realized it was possible to walk that route without seeing another human being and without visiting any village or hamlet. He then issued a challenge to anyone who could complete the route on foot within twenty-four hours, a distance of forty-two miles. He achieved that himself. That was in 1955 and now the Lyke Wake Walk has become part of moorland lore with thousands of people completing the crossing either alone or in organized parties.

Most complete the trek well within the twenty-four hour limit but part of the walk is an ancient funeral processional route. In ancient times, it was believed the souls of the dead went up to Whinney Moor high on the hills hereabouts, and then on to the Bridge of Death and beyond. The Cleveland Lyke Wake Dirge was sung during the processionals, the word 'lyke' referring to the corpse (from which we get lych-gate, under which coffins would pass or rest on their way into church) and the word 'wake' meaning the vigil over a dead body. Thus a *lyke wake* was the vigil over the body of a deceased person and because the route of this walk makes partial use of that old funeral route, it seemed fitting to name it *Lyke Wake Walk.*

The ancient dirge was known in various forms throughout the north of England, with Sir Walter Scott using his own version. In the North York Moors, it was probably last used around 1800, but there is a reference to it in 1686 when John Aubrey wrote, 'The beliefe in Yorkshire was among the vulgar (perhaps is in part still) that after a person's death the soule went over Whinney Moor' and till about 1616–24, at the funerals, a woman came and sang the following song: (There are ten verses, but I will quote only three).

This yah neet, this yah neet,
Ivvery neet an' all,
Fire an' fleet an' cannle leet,
An' Christ tak up thy soul.

When thoo frae hence away art passed,
Ivvery neet an' all,
Ti Whinney Moore thoo cums at last,
An' Christ tak up thy soul.

If ivver thoo gave owther hosen or shoon,
Ivvery neet an' all,
Clap thee doon an' put 'em on,
An' Christ tak up thy soul.

In modern times, some of the walkers chant all ten

awesome verses as they attempt the crossing but I knew that some adopted other means of completing the Lyke Wake Walk – one rode across on a cycle, two went across as if in a three-legged race, others ran across – and I had heard of a team actually carrying a coffin the full length of that route. So was that coffin the relic of another such attempt? If those lads had been carrying it across the moors, and one had then been taken ill, it seemed logical they would dump or hide it somewhere, probably in a place they hoped it would not be found, until they could retrieve it. That seemed a logical answer.

'Which taxi did they ring, Eric? Any idea?'

'There's a number next to the phone,' he told me. 'It's a public phone in the corridor that leads to the toilets. If they ring that taxi firm, they get a free call.'

I went to the phone and rang; it was Swift Taxis of Ashfordly and it didn't take long for me to establish that the two lads had been taken to Dr William Williams, the fiery Welsh doctor with a practice in Ashfordly. I thanked my contact, thanked Eric and decided to visit Dr Williams on my way back to Aidensfield. When I arrived about half an hour later, surgery had finished and the doctor was out on his rounds, but his receptionist could confirm that two men had visited the doctor the previous night, one of whom was suspected of suffering from appendicitis. He was taken to Galtreford Cottage Hospital by ambulance, and his pal had accompanied him. She told me their names were Giles Hamilton and Geoffrey Walshaw, both from Durham; the sick man was Giles Hamilton.

Although the presence of the coffin was not a high priority police matter, and probably not even my responsibility, I did want to bring the affair to a satisfactory conclusion, if only for my own peace of mind. As Galtreford, a small market town rather like Ashfordly, was now part of our enlarged section, it was perfectly feasible for me to pay it a visit on duty, and so I did, my purpose being to see if Giles Hamilton was still in hospital. When I arrived at the reception desk and explained my purpose, I was allowed into the ward to speak to Giles, even though it was not during official visiting hours. The uniform achieved that for me! I asked the nurse to warn him of my impending visit so that my arrival would not be too alarming and established that he had had an emergency operation during the night for appendicitis and was now recovering.

When I went to his bedside, I found a very worried-looking man who would be in his late twenties, bearded and fresh-faced and so I sat on the chair and tried to appear as friendly as I could. Uniformed police officers arriving like this, especially in a hospital, were generally less than friendly, I knew!

'You are Giles Hamilton?' I began.

'Yes,' and he looked dreadfully worried and concerned.

'I'm PC Rhea from Aidensfield,' I introduced myself. 'You're not in trouble, Giles, I just think you might help me solve a puzzle.'

'Oh, well, right, yes, if I can. Is it about the coffin?' and I could see the beginnings of a smile on his face. The coffin was obviously his and its fate had clearly been bothering him.

'Spot on!' I laughed.

'I wondered what might happen if we left it there, we thought it was well hidden but it was dark when we shoved it into that bracken . . . there was no way I could continue carrying it, I was nearly bent double with pain.'

I explained how I had come to be involved and the steps I had taken to trace him, adding that so far as I was concerned the coffin could remain there as long as necessary – jokingly, I told him I did not consider it could be classified as litter and so I had no intention of reporting him for dumping it! In return, he explained how he and Geoffrey Walshaw had decided to tackle the Lyke Wake Walk while carrying a coffin. He added the coffin was jointly owned by he and Geoffrey; they'd had it specially made.

They were not carrying it across the moors for a dare or as a publicity stunt, not even as a charity fund-raising exercise; it was nothing more than a harmless bit of fun which hadn't quite worked out due to his attack of appendicitis.

'So what's happening to the coffin?' I asked. 'Do you want me to arrange for it to be collected and stored where it will be safe? It could be recorded officially as found property!'

'It's good of you but no thanks, Geoffrey's already gone to arrange something,' he said. 'He's got a pal in Ashfordly who's got a van and the idea is to collect it sometime today and take it back to his place. When I'm fit enough, I hope we can have another crack at doing the Lyke Wake Walk, complete with coffin. That's the idea. We're determined to walk the full route while carrying a coffin!'

'Well, good luck to you,' I smiled as I prepared to leave. 'I won't make any entries in any of my official records and certainly won't classify it as found property, but at least I can tell Mr Marshall the story when he rings me later.'

Giles laughed, adding, 'There's just one problem when we do eventually complete our coffin walk, Mr Rhea – we can't leave it on the moors so what can we do with a redundant coffin?'

'You could always dig a hole and bury it,' I suggested.

Continuing the theme of death and coffins, misers are always fascinating if only for their deviousness and the desperate, and at times remarkable, measures they take to avoid spending money, even on essentials like food, heat and clothing.

One hears many stories of such people; typical are those who never spend money on themselves, their homes, their relations or friends, and who then die leaving many hundreds of thousands of pounds which either goes to the taxman or to a cats' home. It is always a tragedy that such misers can never enjoy their money or permit others to enjoy it although, of course, I am aware that their enjoyment comes from counting their hoarded pennies and taking every possible step to avoid expenditure, even to the extent of blowing out candles before they burn away too much of the wick and saving burnt matches in case they can be re-used.

History has produced some noteworthy misers, one of whom was Sir Hervey Elwes who died in 1763 to leave the then enormous sum of £250,000. He never spent more than £110 in a year but his sister-in-law inherited £100,000 and starved herself to death because she did not like spending money on heating and food while her son, a wealthy brewer, never cleaned his shoes, never bought new clothes and also did his utmost to avoid spending money on food. Even so, they pale in comparison with Hetty Howland Green who died in 1916 to leave $95 million. She had more than $31 million cash in one bank account alone. She ate cold porridge because she did not want to spend money on heating it, while her son had to have his leg amputated because she took too long finding a medical clinic who would treat him free of charge.

On my patch at Aidensfield, which included several other small villages, there were several people, men and women, who might be classified as misers, albeit not in the league of those mentioned above.

A dictionary definition of a miser is one who lives miserably in order to hoard wealth (*New Penguin English Dictionary*, 2000). That decription fits misers the world over and I have already chronicled some of the deeds and misdeeds of local misers in previous volumes. But Ebenezer Slyman was perhaps the most devious of all. And one of the most mean.

Ebenezer lived in a ramshackle cottage in Waindale, a tiny hamlet deep in the moors. Its exterior was always in need of paint and minor repairs, the garden was never tended while filthy thin curtains were always draped at the equally filthy windows. The curtains were never closed but never fully open either – they seemed always to be at the halfway stage but lights never appeared inside the house. Ebenezer was too mean to switch on any of his electric lights, to fill his oil lamps with paraffin or to keep his candles burning one second longer than necessary. I think he went to bed early to avoid paying for heat and light. He never ventured out to the shops, he had no means of transport other than his feet, and I learned, in time, that some of the villagers would take him food or buy him provisions from local shops. The local postmaster called on occasions but only to hand over Ebenezer's old age pension. His exact age was not known to anyone, except perhaps the postmaster who would know his date of birth from his pension book but it was generally accepted he was well over eighty and even approaching ninety. The only view that most of us gained was a fleeting glimpse of a shaggy grey haired, bearded face which would sometimes appear at one of the windows, as if waiting for someone to arrive. We guessed that that someone would probably be one of his kindly benefactors.

There is no doubt that many villagers thought Ebenezer had no money and existed in dire poverty but in fact, according to some who knew his relations, he was extremely wealthy. It was claimed he had inherited a huge sum from a rich bachelor uncle but no one was quite sure how much was involved. I recall the figure of £3 million being mentioned – a massive amount in the 1960s – but, of course, had no guarantee it was an accurate assessment. No one knew whether other members of Ebenezer's family had been left a share of that wealth and no one knew why that uncle had left him so much. One theory was that the uncle was also a miser of remarkable skill who thought Ebenezer would not fritter away his inheritance. I don't think Ebenezer drew money from the bank because he never left the cottage and never asked anyone else to obtain the cash for him, other than his pension from the village post office. I did hear he used cheques for things like his rates, electricity account and so forth and I also knew that the local shopkeeper from Elsinby would sometimes make a delivery to his home. In those cases, he paid with a larger-than-necessary cheque and was given his change in cash. That way, he always had cash in the house – without necessarily spending it. An alternative story was that he kept all his money hidden in the cottage. In cash. I doubted that – several million pounds in cash would require a lot of concealment but Ebenezer was highly skilled at hiding his money. Most of us were sure Ebenezer did keep a substantial amount of money somewhere in his cottage – a man like him would never spend all the cash brought by the shopkeeper and postmaster, so it was almost a certainty it was hidden somewhere in his cottage. Certainly, he had more cash coming into the house than going out.

As a policeman, I worried that rumours of such a hoard, whether genuine or not, might reach the ears of local villains who would have no qualms about raiding the cottage in their search for easy pickings but in my time at Aidensfield, there were no reported burglaries or housebreakings at Ebenezer's cottage.

In spite of the speculation about his background, not a great deal was really known about his private life. He had no known interests except his books – and he had a massive collection of volumes on shelves around the house and stacked on almost every surface in most rooms, even on the steps of his staircase. No one knew how he had acquired these – perhaps they were also a family inheritance? Whatever their origins, they could be seen through the curtains and on occasions, Ebenezer could be seen sitting in his armchair with an open book on his lap.

Apart from that, he seemed to have no other interests but the villagers were sure he had never been married although, according to local intelligence, he had younger brothers and sisters living in the York area. He never visited them because it would cost money to travel to York, and he never invited them to his home because that would also involve expenditure on things like telephone calls, postage, writing materials, heat, light and food. It was known that a younger brother called Aaron called to see him about twice a year but the fact he had other brothers and sisters – the exact number being unknown – meant he was also likely to have nephews and nieces, or even great nephews and great nieces. Of this quite large family, only Aaron appeared to keep in touch.

And so it was that Ebenezer Slyman lived as a recluse or hermit, apparently quite content in his own little world in which money need not be unnecessarily spent and in which visiting people did not pressurize him into parting with his money. And then one day, a man arrived in Waindale to seek the home of Ebenezer Slyman. By chance, I was in the village dealing with the renewal of a firearms certificate. I had called at a house in the main street and the postmaster, who operated the recently-opened post office from his own front room, spotted me as I left.

'Nick,' Tony Hepworth called out to me. 'Nick, I might be poking my nose into other people's affairs, but I've just had a chap call at the post office to ask for directions to Ebenezer's house. Only minutes ago. I couldn't refuse him, he could be legitimate, but he's a stranger and Ebenezer never has visitors except Aaron and local tradesmen. I thought you should know. He had a car, by the way, it's along there now.'

'Thanks, Tony, I'll check him out.'

If I could obtain the car's registration number, I could check the identity of its owner and so I decided to walk towards Ebenezer's cottage. As I turned the corner, I could see a car parked outside; it was a pale blue and cream Hillman estate car and I noted its number. Obtaining the owner's name and address from that number could not be achieved speedily at that time – the usual method was to depatch a Form HO/RT/1 by post to the relevant vehicle registration authority but the response could take a few days, although in emergencies it could be done by telephone.

In that day's case, it meant a radio call to the duty constable at Ashfordly Police Station who in turn would ring the registration authority who would then make a search in their files but such action was usually taken only in emergencies. I did not think this was an emergency, not yet – but I did have the number and that was an important piece of information. The technique here, I felt, was not to attempt to obtain the fellow's name and address by that means but to confront him and ask him to prove his identity and state his purpose for being here. I could do that on the grounds I was keeping a watchful eye on Ebenezer's welfare. When I approached the house, the door was closed but I could see the visitor clearly inside, so I decided to be bold and intrusive, if only because I did not want Ebenezer to come to any harm. I knocked and within a few seconds, the door was opened by a man in a smart dark suit and an air of efficiency about him.

'Yes? Oh, it's the police . . . not trouble, I hope,' he frowned as he studied me. As we stood facing one another, I could see Ebenezer in the background darkness of the entrance hall; he was also regarding me with some suspicion.

'No, I hope not,' I felt rather uncomfortable at the situation in which I now found myself but told myself I was doing my duty to protect a vulnerable member of the public. 'I'm PC Rhea, the local policeman, I keep an eye on Ebenezer, we all do, the people in the village that is, and I was just checking he's all right.'

'Ah!' the man was quick-thinking. 'My car . . . a visitor . . . a stranger in the village . . . a newcomer knocking on a vulnerable old man's door . . . everyone's wondering what's going on, that sort of thing!'

'Just routine,' I heard myself trot out the well-used police excuse for what appear to be intrusive actions.

'I'm not complaining, officer, in fact I'm pleased someone is keeping an eye on him even if he doesn't want it! I'm Derek Slyman, his nephew; well, great nephew to be precise, his youngest brother's grandson,' and he delved into his breast pocket to pull out a business card which was lodged between the pages of his driving licence. He handed both to me – and so saved me the embarrassment of asking for some proof of identification. I saw his name and address on both but did not record any of the details. I saw his name was Derek Slyman and he lived in York; his business card said he was the sales director for a firm of bedroom furniture manufacturers. 'Thanks,' I said. 'I won't trouble you further.'

'Look, I know the whole family will appreciate the way you all keep an eye on him, he's always kept us at bay, all through the years except my grandad, never wanting us to call, never visiting us, never buying Christmas cards or presents, but we thought it was time we took the initiative and reminded him he does have a family!'

'We knew he had brothers and sisters in the York area, but no one here seems to know them.'

'That's not surprising, with him living like a hermit. Anyway, PC Rhea, I can tell you this because it's something you should know. It's his birthday, you see, in a couple of month's time. He'll be ninety and I'm trying to get him to agree to some kind of family celebration, either here in a local hotel or village hall, or even at York. I'd willingly come to collect him – so that's what this all about.'

'Thanks, we knew he was getting on a bit!'

'From the way he lives and denies himself things, it's

amazing he's survived this long. I'm telling you because there might be a lot of coming and going over the next few days and weeks, maybe not only me but some of his other relations . . . and if I know him, he won't be the most co-operative of people. He might even lock us out! But we're determined to celebrate his big birthday, with him there if we can. We'd rather have a happy family occasion instead of gathering like vultures at his funeral.'

'Thanks for being so open with me, I'll tell Tony at the post office and he'll make sure the villagers know. But I think it's a great idea. And the best of luck for your plans!'

And as Derek Slyman disappeared back indoors to use his salesman's persuasive techniques upon a very stubborn great uncle, I returned to acquaint Tony with this unexpected development in the life of Waindale's miser. Tony thanked me and explained that he had earlier met Derek's grandfather who was a quiet, nervous sort of man, hardly the type to persuade Ebenezer to do something against his wishes. That's probably why the more worldly Derek had been persuaded by his family to attempt the impossible – i.e. to prise Ebenezer from his home and get him to spend a few pounds enjoying a party with his relations.

Over the following weeks, Derek was a frequent visitor to Ebenezer's cottage, usually bringing things like food and even some new clothes, and he also spent time tidying the garden and smartening the exterior of the house. All at his own expense, of course. Ebenezer would regard it all as a waste of good money.

Derek also kept in touch with Tony at the post office, explaining that these activities were his contribution towards his great uncle's welfare although he did make it known that the ulterior motive was to chip away at old

Ebenezer's resistance and persuade him to attend the birthday party. Whenever Derek or Tony saw me in the village, they would update me on the latest in this domestic saga and so it was that I learned the party was to be held at a smart hotel in York, on the actual date of Ebenezer's birthday. The entire hotel had been taken over by the family, with some travelling from distant places; they could be residents while the more local relatives could attend on the day. A splendid dinner had been arranged followed by music and dancing in the hotel's ballroom. It was a fitting celebration for a man of wealth – the only uncertainty being whether or not Ebenezer would actually attend.

A bedroom had been reserved in his name, however, and the plan was that his youngest brother, Aaron, would drive over to Waindale on the morning of the grand celebration and transport Ebenezer to the York hotel. Aaron, in his late seventies, was perhaps his most frequent visitor and the person most in touch with him over the years. If anyone knew Ebenezer's innermost secrets, it would be him, and he would be the one to make the final persuasive move to actually get Ebenezer out of his house and into a car. Derek would be busy at the hotel, finalizing the plans.

I remember wondering who was going to pay for all this splendour and it was Derek who told me that everyone was paying an equal contribution for the meal and dancing and those staying in the hotel had agreed to pay their own costs. I wondered how Derek had persuaded Ebenezer to meet his own costs!

Derek, a salesman, must have been very persuasive because Ebenezer was far too mean to spend any money on frivolous things like parties and unnecessary food or clothes for himself or anyone else. I think that deep down, family members were hoping Ebenezer would confound everyone by offering to pay for the entire party – after all, he was about to become ninety very soon, he can't have many more years to go before the grim reaper mowed him down, he had a fortune hidden away somewhere and after a lifetime of miserliness, some felt he might have a twinge of conscience for all his past meanness. After all, he couldn't take his money with him. From what Derek told me during our chats, I gained the impression that family members were convinced Ebenezer would surprise everyone on the day by a most uncharacteristic display of generosity.

From snippets of intelligence which oozed from the cottage, it seemed that Derek's ministrations had produced some kind of change in Ebenezer's attitude. There was little doubt he had given Derek the impression that he would, albeit somewhat grudgingly, attend the party and meet all his relations. In fact, as the grand occasion grew nearer, the old man was even beginning to sound enthusiastic. The notion of a wonderful meal in the grandeur of a fine hotel was apparently beginning to appeal to Ebenezer – or so he led Derek to believe. But Derek, pushing the plans along with renewed enthusiasm, had not reckoned with Ebenezer's guile. And, even worse, Ebenezer had not taken into account his brother Aaron's guile. In matters of money and subterfuge, one was almost as bad as the other, but in differing ways.

I can only speculate as to precisely what occurred in Ebenezer's cottage on the day of his birthday because no one was there, apart from Ebenezer and later in the day, his brother, Aaron. From what I learned afterwards, however, I think this is what happened.

As the family was preparing to gather in York, Derek was

already at the hotel, liaising with the staff, preparing the seating plan for dinner, making sure all the family residents had a bedroom, checking the situation with the birthday cake and candles, and generally fulfilling his busy role as organiser. The first guests were expected between 2 p.m. and 4 p.m. which gave them time to settle in and prepare for this evening's grand occasion; they were asked to assemble in the bar at 6 p.m. for pre-dinner drinks and a private room had been reserved at 7.30 p.m. for dinner and dancing.

At three that afternoon, Aaron arrived at Waindale in his car to collect Ebenezer and drive him to York. When he reached the door of the cottage it was closed as it always was but Aaron had a key, a Yale, and so he let himself in. That was his usual practice because Ebenezer rarely answered knocks unless he was expecting the caller. Once inside, there was no sign of Ebenezer.

'Eb, you there?' he called from the hallway. 'It's me, Aaron, it's time to go.'

No reply.

Thinking his brother might be out in the garden or perhaps in the bathroom, Aaron searched the ground floor of the cottage and garden without finding any sign of Ebenezer, and then decided to check upstairs, beginning with the bedroom.

And there he found Ebenezer lying in bed with the look of death about him, pale and still. A candle was burning at the bedside – and in life, Ebenezer would never have left a candle to burn unnecessarily. Such expense was totally unjustified which meant that the burning candle clearly indicated that something dramatic and unforeseen had occurred.

'Eb?' Aaron called his name and leant down to listen for signs of breathing but there were none. Ebenezer had died peacefully in his bed. 'Eb, can you hear me? It's Aaron, I've come to take you to the party.'

There was not a flicker of life, no fluttering eyelids, no breathing. Nothing. Aaron reached out to touch his brother's cheek but it was still warm . . . clearly, the old man had only recently passed away.

'Eb, I don't know if you can hear me, but I must get back and tell the others, we can't cancel the party, not now and I'm sure you want us to celebrate your birthday rather than your death. It'll be a few minutes before I leave, I want to compose myself, this is a shock, a great shock . . . I'll pop in again before I go.'

And so Aaron went downstairs – but he had not been fooled. He knew Ebenezer was not dead which was why he had spoken to the 'corpse'. Ebenezer was faking his death so that he would not have to attend the party and would not have to incur any expense . . . and if Aaron called the doctor, then Ebenezer would show that he was alive and well, and that he'd merely been sleeping. But Aaron had no intention of calling the doctor, not yet.

There was another matter to consider.

If Ebenezer died without making a will (which was something he would never do), then his brothers and sisters would inherit his vast wealth. Aaron reasoned that any money in the house, at the time of Ebenezer's death, could be used by those relatives. And he was probably the only person who knew where Ebenezer concealed his cash. It was something he had discovered during his previous visits. All his collected coins were in a large cavity beneath the floor boards in the kitchen but notes such as fivers, pound notes and ten shilling notes were hidden between the pages of books in Ebenezer's extensive library. There were hundreds of books . . .

And so Aaron scuttled around the house, abstracting scores of notes from between the pages of books and stuffing them into a brown paper carrier bag. He had no idea how much he harvested but he made sure there was enough to cover the entire cost of tonight's party. Ebenezer would pay, whether or not he liked, and whether or not he attended! Aaron's logic was that he was not doing anything wrong or criminal because if Ebenezer was truly dead, then that is precisely what would happen to the money. And Ebenezer clearly wanted Aaron to believe he was dead . . .

Quietly proud of his initiative, Aaron went back upstairs and spoke to the 'corpse' which hadn't moved; the candle was still burning, a sure sign that Ebenezer had passed quietly away. Had he been alive, he would have extinguished the candle, a continuing sign of his death – or so he wanted Aaron to believe.

'I'm going now, Eb,' he said to the still form. 'I'll tell the others and will call the doctor, he'll see to things. I'll lock up on the way out and will be back tomorrow to sort out the funeral arrangements.'

And so Aaron left the house with a bag of money for tonight's party while Ebenezer remained in his bed, not daring to move or blow out the candle until he felt sure the coast was clear. I am sure he congratulated himself on his cunning; he had avoided the party and had avoided spending any money. He did consider ringing the doctor to say he'd been ill but was better now – just in case Aaron happened to call out the doctor – but he had no telephone and didn't feel justified in spending money in the village kiosk. So he would deal with the doctor if and when he arrived. No doctor arrived because Aaron did not call him and it was that which perhaps drew Ebenezer's attention to the fact that his ruse had probably been rumbled. But that was of no consequence because he had cleverly avoided any expenditure on his birthday.

In York that night, there was a grand party. Aaron told the guests that Ebenezer had generously decided to pay all the costs even if he could not attend and so an extremely good time was had by all. Everyone wished Ebenezer a very happy ninetieth birthday in his absence, and they drank to his health in the expectation of another fine party when he reached his centenary.

Derek told me this tale but I have no idea whether Ebenezer ever realized that a considerable sum of money had been removed from between the pages of his books but he never made any complaint of theft to me. However, I was told that he had worried himself sick about that bedside candle burning unnecessarily for so long near his 'death' bed. And then I realized he didn't spend his spare time reading his books – he was probably counting the money tucked between their pages.

Chapter 6

It was the poet Robert Burns who reminded us that the best laid schemes of mice and men often go astray and this was certainly the case in the occasional activities of some residents of Aidensfield and district. For unknown reasons, nothing ever seemed to work out properly for some people. Whether this was due to a lack of careful planning, a too-casual approach to the project in mind or merely bad luck is something we may never know but examples included the man who began to fell a tree in his garden, only to have it fall in a direction exactly opposite to what he intended – and it flattened his greenhouse. Another tree feller managed to destroy a neighbour's henhouse while a third blocked a busy road with his amateurish forestry work.

There was one man who tried to increase the space inside his house by knocking down the wall between the living room and kitchen – and part of the upper floor collapsed. Cars have run away because their handbrakes were not set properly, chimneys have caught fire because people threw petrol, not paraffin on a stubborn blaze, people have been swept away at sea in rubber dinghies while snoozing and cattle have escaped into village centres or on to busy roads because ramblers have left farm gates open. In previous volumes, I have related accounts of people diverting moorland streams only to find they have re-routed them through someone's home; I have been told of illicit lovers in cars on the beach who have been caught by the rising tide and there was the pair of naked lovers whose van ran away with them inside to finally crash and set on fire an entire hillside of bracken and young fir trees.

It's all good fun for the police and other agencies for such incidents can happen anywhere in our wonderful country. Gatherings of police officers, firemen, social workers and others love to relate their personal stories of people who are amazingly daft and careless in their personal behaviour. It is perhaps a good thing that although the rescue agencies and public services spend valuable time and money on some spectacular rescues, they are able to laugh about some of them afterwards even if the episode was somewhat embarrassing for the hapless participants. Police canteens are always a rich source of such tales, and it has been said that police officers spend much of their time working as dustmen, i.e. clearing up the mess caused by the great British public.

The truth is that no one is immune from making silly mistakes; we all do so from time to time but most of us manage to contain our embarrassment within the family circle, like the man who forgot to place his order for milk outside one night and got up very early next morning to do so. The snag was that he was naked and as he stepped outside to postion his empty bottle on the doorstep, the door slammed shut due to a strong draught, the Yale latch dropped and he was marooned in the street, completely naked. Luckily, it was very early and almost dark, so no one saw him; his wife responded to his urgent cries and he was hurriedly returned to the safety of his home.

Even if many of us do silly things from time to time, there are others who would claim they have never made a fool of themselves. Such a man was Christopher Gregory Bentham, a resident of Aidensfield.

He was one of the most organized of people, seemingly living his life to carefully prepared and well-thought-out plans. In his early sixties, he was a tall, slim and very smart silver-haired gentleman of impressively neat appearance. He was always immaculately dressed in the most up-to-date of stylish clothes, he never had a hair out of place and his shoes were always shining. Razor sharp creases always adorned his trousers; his shirt sleeves, with diamond cufflinks, appeared below those of his jacket by precisely the right length and his tie was always perfectly adjusted. Not a tiny piece of dust, hair or dandruff would ever dare to attach itself to his smart dark suits and he would never allow his pockets to bulge with unsightly contents.

In addition to his personal appearance, his large detached stone-built house was similarly perfect and handsome on its elevated site along Elsinby Road. The windows were always shining and clean, the paintwork scrubbed, the gutters devoid of leaves and the paths weedless and rubbish free. His garden was a picture with a lawn as green and smooth as a bowls pitch, borders which had no idea what a weed looked like and a vegetable garden which might have been an advertisement for an horticultural catalogue. It was said that if Christopher Gregory grew daffodils, they would all bloom while facing the same direction; if he grew potatoes, they would rise in regimented lines and if he grew apples, pears or plums, they would all be of a uniform size and shape. Perfection in all things was what Christopher Gregory sought – and by all accounts, achieved. And that philosophy extended to his wife.

It must be said that Mrs Bentham – Cynthia – complemented and matched her husband in all things.

Beautifully dressed and coiffeured with an elegance not usually associated with ladies from a rustic background, she looked and behaved like a model. Tall and slender, she walked with an easy grace and even if the street was wet and muddy, she could navigate the perils it presented in such style that her shoes never got dirty and her stockings never got splashed. She was always pleasant to others, always willing to help at village events and always pleasant to meet. And if this handsome couple were perfection itself, they just happened to be very nice people indeed. They were not snobbish, they did not speak with what the Yorkshire folks called a posh accent and they were happy to join village events, to help whenever required and to pop into the pub for a drink or a bar snack. They were very good mixers, affable, a delight to talk to and welcome at any event regardless of class.

Beyond doubt, they were lovely, kind and charming people, a credit to Aidensfield; Christopher Gregory was a solicitor by profession with an office in Ashfordly while Cynthia ran a small secretarial agency with clients in the business world. Her office was also in Ashfordly. Speaking as the village constable, I knew that the community was very happy they had chosen to live among us.

However, no one is perfect no matter how hard they try and in the case of the Benthams, it was Cynthia who had a slight character defect. She liked to drop names. When meeting people in the street or on social occasions, she had a habit of just happening to mention she had been talking recently to a famous author, television personality, actor or actress, politician, top-flight businessman or woman or some other person in the public eye, even members of the royal family.

She had actually spoken to the Queen on one memorable occasion, so we were told, and had been seated next to Winston Churchill at some gathering a few years before he died in 1965. Then, on a business trip to America, she had actually walked into a restaurant in New York just as President Kennedy was leaving. His smile had caused her heart to flutter like a trapped butterfly, so she told everyone, especially when she was allocated his vacated table.

She'd had a drink with Vivian Nicholson, the Yorkshire pools winner who said she was going to 'spend, spend, spend'; she'd once been on the same cross-channel ferry as Bruce Forsyth, and had shaken hands with every member of both the Rolling Stones and Beatles pop groups, meeting the Beatles when they performed at Scarborough in December, 1963. To hear her chatter in her wide social circles, one might believe she knew everyone of importance throughout the world, and was close friends with many of them.

When she made it known she was the cousin of Laurie Willshaw, the high profile Yorkshire and England cricketer, however, people smiled and nodded, as if believing this was just perhaps another of her many fantasies. Shortly before his well-publicised retirement from first-class cricket, Willshaw was in the headlines because he had achieved some remarkable feats. Playing in a county match against Nottinghamshire, he had scored 36 runs off a six-ball over, a feat matched later only by Sir Garfield Sobers in 1968 and

Ravishankar Jayadritha Shastri in 1985. Willshaw had also scored six successive centuries in six county matches and had once scored fifty runs in less than nine minutes while batting against Kent.

His achievements with a cricket bat, all attained within the same 1964 season, had made him almost a national hero. Cynthia's claims happened to coincide with Willshaw's well-publicised announcement that he was going to retire from first-class cricket, and so it was that the Yorkshire County Cricket Club announced he would be playing some testimonial matches around the county prior to his departure.

By another happy coincidence, the captain of the Aidensfield village cricket team, Rob Allanby, also announced he was going to retire at the end of the same season and the club chairman, our local auctioneer Rudolph Burley, thought it might be an idea if he also had a testimonial match as his farewell. After all, he had been captain for the last twenty years, he had led his team to many outstanding victories while nurturing some very good cricketers but he was now well past the normal playing age. For lots of reasons, therefore, he deserved a proper farewell.

It was then that Rudolph, chatting at the bar of the pub with Oscar Blaketon as I was enjoying a quiet pint beside them, suddenly said, 'I wonder if Cynthia could persuade Laurie Willshaw to play at Rob's testimonial match? If he did make an appearance, it would draw a big crowd. We'd have a healthy pot of cash to celebrate Rob's retirement and it would make a memorable occasion for the village.'

'I don't know about that,' Blaketon was as cautious as ever. 'Do you think she really is his cousin? I mean, Rudolph, it seems she's met or talked to every famous person that's walked this earth. I reckon she's romancing just a little now that he's never out of the headlines.'

'I've always thought she was genuine,' I felt I should make a contribution to this discussion. 'I know she never misses a chance to drop names, but I've no reason to think she's lying. And her maiden name was Willshaw, I saw it on an old driving licence when she produced her current one to me a few months ago.'

'Well, there's only one way to find out!' smiled Rudolph. 'I'll go and see her to ask if she can persuade her famous cousin Laurie to play cricket in Aidensfield.'

'Fat chance he'll agree!' chortled Blaketon.

It was a few days later when I spotted Rudolph walking towards the post office and so I took the opportunity to ask about Cynthia's response.

'She was full of enthusiasm,' he told me. 'She rang him and he said he would consider the idea once his diary of commitments was fixed; it seems there's a family wedding in May, in Herefordshire and she'll expect to see him there. He's promised to give his answer then so we'll have to wait a little longer. If he does come, though, he said it would have to be towards the end of the season, he's got a lot of important fixtures to accommodate during the summer months.'

'Well, it all sounds very promising,' I had to admit. 'So it's a case of wait and see.'

The outcome was that Laurie Willshaw agreed to come to Aidensfield to play in a local match for the benefit of Rob Allanby. He confirmed the date which was to be the second Saturday in September, adding that Aidensfield Cricket Club would not be faced with any expenditure because Laurie would be accommodated by the Benthams.

He was more than happy that the occasion be used as a testimonial match for Rob Allanby with all the attendant efforts to raise funds such as an entrance fee, a raffle, a fair-ground, stalls selling cakes, crafts and so forth, an ice cream van, a splendid cricket tea, invited guests and anything else which might produce a happy and enjoyable occasion. And, of course, he agreed that the match be played on Aidensfield cricket ground, that publicity be given to the event and that its precise format be left to the discretion of members of Aidensfield cricket club. Laurie said he would cheerfully do whatever was required on the day, suggesting perhaps that an exhibition of his batting prowess be considered or even that he took part in a local match. He made it known to Cynthia, who really was his cousin, that a local match was probably the best idea because it allowed all the players to compete with him on equal terms, either when batting, bowling or fielding.

This exciting development created intense interest in the locality and as members of the cricket club discussed the best way of accommodating this world-class batsman, so supporters began to organize events which would take place in the outfield surrounding the pitch. Thanks to advance publicity in the local papers, keen interest was shown by lots of volunteer entertainments such as a local fair complete with shooting gallery, dodgems and rides for the children, along with the WI cake stall, guess the weight of the pig and an entire panapoly of fun so that the whole day promised to become something of a festival rather than a mere cricket match. All the proprietors of outside entertainments and stalls would pay a fee to the cricket club for use of the field and so a useful sum of money was assured for Rob Allanby.

So far as Laurie Willshaw's participation was concerned,

it was decided that a variation of a normal cricket match would be staged, but it would remain a contest between the Aidensfield first eleven and the Aidensfield second eleven. Because of Laurie's skill as a batsman, it was decided the game should be of twenty overs for each side which meant it would be completed during the course of the afternoon with an air of increased excitement. Furthermore, it was also decided that Laurie would play in his usual county place, i.e. number three in the batting order, but here was the difference – he would bat for both sides, and if that meant more than the usual eleven players on each side, then it did not matter. It was just a bit of fun after all. What did matter was that Laurie was given ample opportunity to demonstrate his undoubted skills in a village cricket environment. With twenty overs being allowed for each side, every team member would be able to bowl at least one over to him.

That modest diversion from the normal meant the vital cricket atmosphere would be maintained whilst allowing every player to show his paces against this famous batsman, either to bowl against him, to act as a fieldsman for his renowned classic strokes and even to run the length of the pitch as the great man scored his runs. It seemed a good idea; Cynthia was asked to present these proposals to Laurie and he agreed, adding that he was looking forward to his visit to the picturesque North York moors and to Aidensfield in particular. Equally, of course, the cricket enthusiasts of the district were looking forward to seeing this fine international ambassador in action on a local cricket field and some local matches were postponed to allow other clubs to enjoy Aidensfield's great day.

It promised to be a wonderful occasion and a large crowd

was expected. As I was an occasional member of the first team, when my police duties allowed, I found myself being asked to play at number seven in the first team and as one of the regular fast bowlers, I would also be expected to bowl an over at Laurie. I felt a glow of pride at this and found myself becoming as excited as the others at the prospects of sharing a game of cricket with Laurie Willshaw. I made sure my whites and boots were in splendid condition for the occasion and then, on a fine warm September afternoon, my family and I made our way to the cricket field. When we arrived, a large crowd had already gathered and the outfield was full of attractions such as the fairground, stalls and childrens' entertainments. Elsinby brass band was playing and I could smell the distinctive aroma of steak and sausages being barbecued. As Mary and the children left to find a suitable vantage position among the crowd, I went to the pavilion to get changed into my cricketing gear and to meet Laurie Willshaw.

He was already there when I arrived, a tall lithe man in his mid-thirties. Tanned, fit and handsome, he had a shock of dark wavy hair, very deep brown eyes and an infectious smile which displayed a set of strong white teeth. He was chatting amiably to everyone, shaking hands, giving advice, asking about the village and generally making himself at home in our modest pavilion. It was evident he was accustomed to mixing with strangers because he took centre stage with the immediate effect of making everyone like him. He displayed not a shred of boastfulness and never a hint of superiority as he settled down to the task of playing a happy game of village cricket.

Ten minutes or so before we were due on to the field, Rudolph Burley called for our attention and made the formal introductions; everyone applauded Laurie when he said how delighted he was to join us today and then Rudolph outlined the plans, giving details of the plan whereby Laurie would play at number three for both teams. The respective openers were asked not to dig themselves in for a long spell because the public had come to see Laurie play, not them, and so they had to make it look as if they were playing a real match but at the same time, make sure they were out, preferably as early as possible. It was hoped that all team members would get a chance to bat alongside Laurie and that all would have a chance to bowl at him. That was the spirit of today's somewhat artificial game.

Then the two captains tossed a coin to determine who should bat first, and the first team won. To loud applause, therefore, the second team walked on to the pitch as fielders while the scoreboard operator prepared her numerals; the umpires checked the stumps and positioned the bails, then examined the ball which was brand new. The opening batsmen inspected the pitch and hammered down imaginary bumps with their bats as the tension and anticipation increased. To add to the atmosphere, a public address system had been installed and Rudolph, in his auctioneer's voice, was commentator. He told the spectators how the match was to be structured and asked for a round of applause for the opening batsmen, Ridley and Kelly, both living in Aidensfield. Heavily padded, they strode out to the wicket to the applause of the expectant crowd. The opening bowler for the second team was to be Eric Scott and so the match got underway to a carnival atmosphere.

A huge cheer arose as Scott bowled the first ball; Ridley connected and they ran a single. Kelly now faced Scott and he tipped the ball to square leg and ran another single. In keeping with the club's wishes, however, neither batsman intended to produce a match winning performance and so, on the final ball of that first over, Ridley managed to lift a delivery into the air so that he was caught at cover point without adding to his score. Now it was the turn of Laurie Willshaw.

He strode out to the wicket amid loud applause and cheers, waving his bat in the air to acknowledge the crowd. He took his stance, called for the umpire to check he was defending the middle stump, looked around to check the position of the fielders and then nodded to the umpire to indicate he was ready. The crowd fell silent.

There was now a change of bowler. In keeping with the plan that every player should bowl at least one over at Willshaw, it was now the turn of the youngest player on the field. It was deemed fitting that he should be the first to bowl at the club's famous guest. The second team permitted lads aged fifteen and upwards to join them – those below that age played for the juniors and Aidensfield did have a good junior team. Today, therefore, it was the privilege of fifteen year old Neil Longster to deliver the first ball to Laurie Willshaw. Neil was a tousle-haired ginger headed lad with a face full of freckles and a sense of mischief which had always got him into trouble at school and elsewhere. Rather stocky in build and perhaps not as tall as other lads of his age, he was a very good all-rounder with some believing he had the potential for a career in professional cricket.

Today, therefore, he found himself in the spotlight as he accepted the ball from the captain and prepared for his first delivery. Now the spectators became very quiet indeed as they watched with keen interest. Neil paced out his run, kicked the turf with his heel to mark the start, turned and began to race towards the point of delivery. Willshaw waited, his eye on the ball and his bat tapping the crease almost to the timing of Neil's feet thudding upon the ground. And then the lad bowled. A fraction of a second later, there was the crack of leather against wood and Willshaw's middle stump was lying flat on the ground as the bails were scattered behind him. England's most famous and skilled batsman had been clean bowled by this ginger haired fifteen year old from Aidensfield.

There was a long silence from the crowd as if they did not believe what they had witnessed and then the umpire's finger was raised to indicate Willshaw was out. He stared at the stumps in evident disbelief but, being a true sportsman, accepted the decision without question as the crowd now began to applaud and cheer – but it was all for young Neil. There was no doubt he had ruined that opportunity for Willshaw to display his skills, but in so doing he had established his own piece of Aidensfield cricketing lore. Then Willshaw did a remarkable thing – before making that long walk back to the pavilion, he strode towards the surprised youngster and shook him by the hand then patted him amiably on the shoulders before raising Neil's hand in the air in a gesture of triumph. The crowd erupted with delight. In those few seconds, Laurie Willshaw did more for his reputation than he would have done with a dazzling display of batsmanship.

It must be said that his second stint at the wicket was more in keeping with our expectations. He produced a remarkable display of professionalism and entertained the crowd with some magical strokes as everyone took part in a thoroughly enjoyable demonstration of the art of cricket. Later, when it was all over and the result was declared a draw, Laurie Willshaw had the grace to admit that Neil's delivery had beaten him. He told us he had not deliberately allowed himself to be bowled out by a youngster and then offered Neil a trial with Yorkshire County Cricket Club, saying he would invite him along as his personal guest.

In all, therefore, it was a wonderful day but even now, no one speaks of Laurie Willshaw's display at the Aidensfield wicket yet they can all remember when young Neil bowled out England's finest batsman with his very first ball. It was a talking point for years afterwards with all manner of people claiming they were actually there to witness it.

Even if Cynthia Bentham's plans did not quite work out as she expected on that occasion, she continued to name drop but for some reason did not mention her famous cousin's name quite so frequently. I wondered if, when Neil Longster became a famous Yorkshire county cricketer, she would tell everyone she knew him? I felt sure she would.

Another person whose plans did not work out quite as expected was John George Watkins, 26 years old, of Flat 1, No. 18, Moorside Close, Ashfordly. He described himself as unmarried and a labourer by profession.

Few if any of John George's plans ever worked out because he could never hold down any kind of regular employment, he was out of work more than he was in work and he was constantly in trouble with the police for petty thefts, fighting, causing disturbances, drunkenness and general lawlessness such as breaking windows, urinating in the street, riding his bike without lights and using obscene language in a public place. His attempts to learn how to drive a car had finished up with him being fined for careless driving, having no insurance or road tax, driving without L plates, taking a motor vehicle without the owner's consent, using a car in a dangerous condition and, in his most recent case, being heavily fined and disqualified for reckless driving. In a borrowed car, he'd driven along the footpath in a busy street because a delivery lorry was blocking the road and as a consequence, he had knocked down and injured two pedestrians. He was still a learner at that time but had been driving without being supervised. He had accumulated dozens of petty convictions from regular appearances before Ashfordly Magistrates' Court and it was known that successive chairmen of the bench had been at a loss as to the best means of dealing with John George. He'd been fined umpteen times, put on probation, bound over to keep the peace and more recently disqualified from driving but he never seemed to learn his lesson. Within weeks of one court appearance, he was behaving in such a way that it was a certainty he would be back in court within a very short time. And he never paid his fines because he never had any money and for that, he had served several short terms of imprisonment – but he had yet to pay those fines.

His parents, a decent couple who lived on a big council estate in Ashfordly, had shown amazing compassion for their troubled son for they had sometimes paid his fines to keep him out of prison but now paid the rent for his flat. It was their way of helping him to cope (and a means of getting him to live away from home) – but of course, he went home regularly for a decent meal and to have his washing done. His long-suffering parents did their best for him and there is no doubt he loved them while at the same time hating himself for being such a disappointment to them – but in the world of the petty criminal, John George could never keep himself out of trouble. I think he did try from time to time – there were some longish gaps in his court appearances – but somehow his resolve never worked. He tooks silly risks and always got arrested. He staggered from one petty crime to another, always getting himself caught or recognized, and invariably finishing up in Ashfordly police cells on yet another charge of some kind. He did make it known that if and when he passed his driving test, he would obtain a job as a driver or delivery man – but his efforts behind the wheel invariably resulted in law-breaking of some kind.

His flat was within a four storey house which was probably Victorian. It had been turned into five flats, one of which was rented to John George for a modest charge. He occupied the basement and his rent was low because his flat also housed the coke fired central heating boiler and water heating boiler. It was his duty to maintain both boilers – the flat owners would make sure the coke was delivered and all that was required of John George was to keep the boilers stoked up and the ash cleaned out. Most of the time, he did that, but sometimes he forgot.

I do know the other residents did their best to remind him! On one occasion, I had to visit him at his flat to question him about the theft of some plant pots from a front garden in town and was pleasantly surprised at its cleanliness and tidiness. He assured me he cared for himself although I suspect his mother came to 'muck him out' from time to time although it was evident he kept himself clean and well groomed. He was not untidy in his dress either. A small wiry man who was quite good at football, he had thick black hair which was always worn long and heavily greased; he had a thin face with dark, darting eyes and long slender fingers which might have been useful had he been a pianist.

He always wore smart dark clothes and shoes with thick soft soles – brothel-creepers as he called them. To speak to him informally was usually a very pleasant experience – he had a certain charm which he could use to good effect and I never heard him be disrespectful to any police officer or others in authority like priests and vicars, the magistrates or even his former school teachers.

For all his charm, it was his propensity for getting himself into trouble that kept John George firmly within the sights of the local police; Ashfordly police officers found themselves visiting his flat on regular occasions or stopping him in the street for a chat to find out what he'd been up to in recent days or weeks and whenever I undertook a spell of duty in town, I would find myself doing likewise.

Then he vanished. We felt there was nothing suspicious about his disappearance but after a while, without John George being sighted at his regular haunts, we learned he had found a job in Scarborough.

His friends and acquaintances told us about it. John George had been offered some kind of seasonal employment at an amusement arcade in Scarborough and it would continue throughout the tourist season. He expected to return to Ashfordly in the autumn. For that reason, he was retaining his flat; his father had promised to pay the rent and keep the boilers stoked up. Quite naturally, all the officers in Ashfordly were delighted. Our crime figures and offence rates would tumble significantly without John George's input and we could relax our vigilance until he returned. I wondered if he would behave himself while in Scarborough.

We heard nothing more of John George until I was undertaking a spell of office duty in Ashfordly Police

Station. It was a hot Wednesday in August and the town was packed with tourists and their cars. Some were visiting the castle, others admiring the shops and cobbled market place and some just enjoying a quiet spell beside the river. Then I received a telephone call from the CID at Scarborough.

'PC Rhea, Ashfordly Police,' I announced.

'Nick my old mate, how are you?' I didn't recognize the voice until he said, 'Andy Piper at Scarborough.'

'Andy! Long time no hear from you!' I joked. We had been on the same initial training course and he was now a detective sergeant in Scarborough. We chatted for a time about our respective lives and then I asked, 'So what can I do for you?'

'Just a routine enquiry,' he said. 'Do you know a man called Kenneth William Carrick of Flat 4, 18, Moorside Close, Ashfordly?'

'Carrick? Sorry, I can't say the name rings a bell.'

At that point, I must admit the significance of the address escaped me. 'We've got him in custody here,' Andy continued. 'He was caught driving a stolen car last night but we're not happy with some aspects of his story, or him! I should really be speaking to your sergeant about this . . .'

'He's on his weekly rest day, Andy. There's just me at the moment.'

'And you've been acting in the rank, I believe?'

'I have, yes.'

'Fair enough, this is a delicate matter.'

'You want me to check that address?'

'Yes please. But Nick, there's more to this than meets the eye. You lads on the beat might not know this man's background but Carrick is a convicted murderer who was jailed for life for killing a woman in Newcastle. He's out on licence now, and he lives at that address.'

'Oh crumbs! So why do you want me to check the address?'

'The character we've got locked up in our cells is about twenty five or thirty at the most. I've checked Carrick's CRO references and he's fifty-six. It means I don't think we've got Carrick in our cells, Nick, I think it's somebody else using his name and confirming it with a stolen driving licence. When we nicked him, he had Carrick's licence on him, you see, but maintained that was his own name and address.'

As he was speaking, my brain was now exercising all kinds of leaps and bounds and then I said, 'Did you say his address is a flat at 18, Moorside Close, here in Ashfordly?'

'That's right.'

'What's he look like?' was my next question.

Andy then described a man who, in my opinion, was the image of John George Watkins.

'Andy, I think the man you've got is really called John George Watkins, a small-time local villain, more of a clown really. He's also got a flat at that address and local intelligence suggests he's working in Scarborough during the tourist season.'

'That makes sense. Living in the same building means he could easily have sneaked into Carrick's flat and nicked his driving licence.'

'It's very likely. Watkins is disqualified, which adds more sense for him to steal a driving licence,' and I provided Andy with the background of John George, relating the driving case which had resulted in his disqualification.

'Right, well first we must check that Carrick is alive and

kicking. And we'll need to know whether he's lost his driving licence. Can you do that immediately if not sooner? And call me back. I'll keep our man in the cells until I hear from you. But you know how we must treat these cases of murderers out on licence. Very discreetly. Much as I would like to frighten the pants off the man in our cells, I daren't tell him he's nicked a murderer's licence . . . that's got to be between our two selves. Your local villain must never know he's got a convicted killer living upstairs.'

I thought it quite hilarious that John George should steal such a person's driving licence and it would have been a salutory lesson for him to be told that if he persisted in claiming he was Carrick, then he faced the rest of a life sentence for breaking the conditions of his release. But I was now faced with a delicate task.

I rang Sub-Divisional Headquarters at Eltering to say I would be out of the office for about an hour on an urgent enquiry, and switched the telephone through to that station. Twenty minutes later, I was climbing the stairs at No. 18, Moorside Close and tapped on the door of Flat 4. I could hear music inside; a radio or record was quietly playing. Then the door was opened, just a fraction, and a rather nervous looking man with grey hair peered out at me.

'Yes?'

'Mr Carrick?'

'Yes.' Clearly he was anxious at being confronted by a uniformed policeman.

'Can I have a word with you?'

'Er, well, yes, I suppose so. You'd better come in.'

He was comfortably dressed in a grey shirt, an old woollen cardigan, grey slacks and slippers, and the radio was playing in the corner of the living room. It was sparsely furnished with tatty old chairs and a table and a gas fire was burning in the grate. He went over and switched off the radio. He looked fifty-five, a grey haired man with a round and rather solemn face, grey eyes and a pale skin. He closed the door behind me but didn't offer me a seat.

'I'm sorry to trouble you,' I began. 'But we have a man in custody at Scarborough police station and he is claiming to be you. In fact, he's got your driving licence.'

'Oh dear . . .' he licked his lips. 'That is dreadful . . . but I am Carrick. Kenneth and William are my forenames,' and he picked up a pile of letters from his mantelpiece and showed me the name and address on them. They were bills, I saw; gas and electricity.

'Have you lost your driving licence?' I asked. 'Or had it stolen?'

'I thought I had misplaced it, officer. With my wallet. I left my wallet on the table over there, some weeks ago now, it hadn't much money in, just a few pound notes and my driving licence. I couldn't find it and assumed I'd misplaced it somewhere.'

'Did you report it to the police?'

'No, I have no wish to make a fuss, officer. I prefer to live quietly, out of the limelight.'

'Well, I need to have you confirm that your licence is missing. And you can also report the theft of your wallet and its contents.'

'No, I'd rather not. Not make a complaint of theft, I mean. After all, I can't prove it was stolen, can I? I shall say it was lost, officer. Yes, I lost my driving licence some time ago but wasn't too concerned because I do not have a car now and would hardly want to use my licence.'

And so I completed a short statement in my pocket book

in which he confirmed his driving licence was missing, believed lost, and he signed it. That would suffice, I knew. I thanked him and left, apologizing for disturbing him and neither of us mentioned his recent past. He did not look like a murderer, but, I asked myself, what does a murderer look like? I wondered about the crime he had committed . . .

Back in the office, I called Andy Piper and told him Kenneth William Carrick was alive and well and living in Flat 4, adding that I was satisfied about his identity and confirming that he had either lost or misplaced his driving licence and wallet some time ago. He could not or would not report it stolen, however, and so Andy could not charge John George with stealing it. He faced plenty of other charges, however, including driving while disqualified, careless driving, stealing a motor vehicle or alternatively taking one without the consent of the owner.

Some time later, Carrick's driving licence was returned to Ashfordly Police Station and I had the job of restoring it to him, against his signature. John George Watkins never knew he had falsely claimed to be a convicted murderer and when he returned to the flat, he would live in the same state of ignorant bliss because we could never allow a man of his character to learn Carrick's secret. There is no telling how he might react. Likewise, when I returned the licence to its rightful owner, I never told him I knew about his earlier crime and imprisonment and he never told me either.

Bearing in mind his past record, John George Watkins got three months imprisonment from Scarborough magistrates and when he came out of prison to return to his flat, his first action was to smash the window of a local pub.

Chapter 7

A number of us, after eating a boiled egg from an egg-cup, will turn over the empty shell, replace it in the cup and smash it with the back of our spoon. Perhaps some of us no longer do this, even if we did so as children. If you remember smashing your egg shell, ask yourself – why did I do it? Or why do I still do it?

The following may provide the answer. Not so long ago, it was common among parents to tell their children to smash empty boiled egg shells in this manner, sometimes adding that it was unlucky not to do so. In fact this practice dates to our belief in witches because it was thought they used empty egg-shells as a means of transport. In this way, they could secretly approach a person to cast an evil spell upon him or her. It was quite a common belief that witches could travel over water in egg-shells too – this arose because witches could appear as other creatures, perhaps as animals or even insects, hence their ability to travel in this way. A tiny insect floating in an upturned egg-shell or occupying one on the compost heap would not mean much to us nowadays but in bygone times, it could cause genuine terror.

On the coast, there was a similar superstition which caused fisherfolk to believe that an egg shell left unbroken after its contents were used could cause local boats to overturn at sea, and even precipitate major shipwrecks. Furthermore, poultry keepers thought it was unlucky to burn an empty egg shell because it would cause their poultry to cease laying.

For all sorts of reasons, therefore, our ancestors averted the troublesome activities of witches by smashing all empty egg shells to render them harmless.

The odd thing is that some of us continue to do so without pausing to question the reason. Our modern society contains many other remnants of former superstitions, perhaps the most curious being modern hospitals which will not allow mixed bunches of red and white flowers into the wards, and local authorities who refuse to number council houses with 13. It was this kind of lingering folk memory which made me determined to trace the source of a strange practice connected with a hill above Gelderslack, one of the villages on my beat. It was a custom known as 'Going to Witch Hill.'

I am not sure when I first became acquainted with this but I can recall a couple of teenagers walking past me in the main street at Aidensfield as I was chatting to one of the local characters. When the couple, who were clearly very much in love with one another, walked past us hand-in-hand, my companion smiled at me and said, 'Ah reckon they'll soon be gahin up ti Witch Hill.'

'Witch Hill?' I asked.

'Aye, up on t'moors ower Gelderslack way, it's where courting couples usually end up,' he grinned. 'That's if they're serious aboot yan another.'

My immediate reaction was that Witch Hill, a place I had never visited, was some kind of romantic beauty spot or vantage point on the heights. I imagined it to be a place which attracted courting couples due to its solitude or privacy because there were many similar locations throughout the North York Moors. They were always popular with visitors, tourists, dog walkers, ramblers and anyone who loved the fresh air and countryside with its wide open spaces and panoramic views.

Many of these locations had been equipped with seats, litter bins and parking areas, often with a visiting ice-cream van hovering hopefully nearby, although some comprised nothing more than a convenient large rock upon which to sit and enjoy some moments of peace while admiring the surrounding landscape. When hearing that old fellow refer to Witch Hill, therefore, I presumed it was another of those beauty spots, even though I had never had reason to visit the place.

I thought nothing more of Witch Hill until PC Alf Ventress rang me from Ashfordly Police Station one spring morning to say a couple of middle aged women on a hiking holiday were three hours overdue at their lodgings. He provided their names and a physical description, adding they had been last sighted on the moors not far from Witch Hill. Although there was no great concern at this stage, I was asked to keep an eye open for them during my routine patrols. If I came across them, I was asked to ascertain that neither was in distress or in need of assistance, and to request them to contact Mrs Freeman at their lodgings to inform her of their immediate plans. As I was on patrol that evening, and because the name of Witch Hill triggered that memory of the young couple's probable destination, I decided to drive out for a look at the site. En route, I could scour the countryside for two missing middle-aged ladies in hiking gear.

It was a slow drive along narrow winding roads up the dale beyond Gelderslack village and although I maintained a look-out for the two ladies, I did not see them. From time to time, I halted at lofty vantage points to scan the countryside with my binoculars but this also failed to locate them.

To reach Witch Hill from the dale below, I had to drive up a very steep moorland track. It was unsurfaced, being nothing more than an ancient packhorse route from Gelderslack up to the moorland heights but it was becoming increasingly used by tourists as a short cut on to the hills while also being popular with horse riders and ramblers. At intervals along the side of the steep track were areas where a vehicle could pull off the highway to park and so I made use of one of them, parked and consulted my map.

According to the map, Witch Hill lay about a hundred and fifty yards to my left. I climbed from the car and made my way towards a piece of ground which rose slightly higher than the nearby moorland. It took a few minutes to fight my way through the tough heather and bracken which was chest high in places, and then I found myself standing on the small mound of earth. It rose some twenty feet or so higher than the surrounding land and was covered with grass which had been shorn smooth by the ever-present sheep. From there, I could enjoy stunning views across the moors and down Gelderslack Dale, but the same views were obtainable from most points in this vicinity. My conclusion was that Witch Hill was not the most prominent or exciting of vantage points, and furthermore it bore no signs of being regularly visited by anyone, certainly not courting couples. There was no bench, no rock which could be used as a seat, no tracks to it; it was nothing more than a grassy pimple within a vast area of moorland. I did stand on its mini-summit, however, to survey the dale below for signs of the two ladies but failed to find them.

I returned to my police van and decided to radio Ashfordly

Police Station to report my location. From such an elevated place, radio reception was very clear and I had no trouble making contact with my sectional station. Alf Ventress thanked me for making the search but added the ladies had since been in touch with their lodgings by telephone; he'd tried to contact me only a few minutes earlier but I had not responded to his calls. I explained I had been tramping across the moor at that time whereupon he said the women had got lost earlier that afternoon but were now safe and well, and were expected to arrive at their lodgings by nine o'clock that evening. I expressed my relief at the outcome and said I would resume my patrol, intending to book off duty at ten o'clock which was the official end of my shift.

That small incident was typical of many similar reports we received during every tourist season but in this case it reached a happy conclusion. I was not angry or upset at having to spend fruitless time searching for those women; they had not deliberately misled the police and the action of their landlady in raising an early alarm was far better than ignoring their absence. Too long a delay in commencing a search could mean the police might find one or other dead or injured in some remote place. In that instance, however, there was a bonus because my modest part in this had taken me to Witch Hill. And, I must admit, I was not very impressed by it. So why would courting couples make the effort to reach this remote and undistinguished place? If indeed they did! It was a long way from anywhere, certainly well off the proverbial beaten track and in looking at it now, there was no indication that anyone ever came here, apart from sheep and grouse.

Clearly, I needed to find out more about the local ritual which, it seemed, was practised by those in love.

In the days and weeks which followed, the puzzle of Witch

Hill was relegated to the back of my mind due to a fairly busy time with family commitments and police duties. I must admit I thought no more about it until I overheard a conversation between four people sitting at a table in Oscar Blaketon's pub. They were two couples, each in their late sixties and all were local people. They were Bob and Elsie Cummings, and Jack and Doris Warner, all pensioners whom I knew fairly well. It was lunchtime and they were enjoying a snack together, probably to celebrate some personal occasion. I had popped in as a matter of routine during my patrol. I was not there to have a social drink because I was on duty, but my purpose was to catch up with local crime-beating gossip. Pubs were always a good source of intelligence about criminal activities in the locality and while I stood in silence as Blaketon attended to a customer, I heard Bob Cummings say,

'. . . and then I went up to Witch Hill and that was it. We got married a year later and we've been as happy as pigs in muck ever since.'

It was the only part of the conversation I overheard and as I was puzzling over its meaning, Bob came to the bar to order more drinks. He stood beside me to place his order and I knew I must not ignore this opportunity to ask if he could enlighten me.

'Now then Constable Nick,' he greeted me with a smile. 'Doing your duty, eh?'

'It's tough!' I laughed. 'It's very hard work, being a village constable, the pressure is terrible!'

'I can see it is,' he grinned while awaiting Blaketon's attention. 'Mind you, I wouldn't have your job for the world, you've got to please everybody and finish up pleasing nobody. You can't do right for doing wrong in the minds of some folks.'

'We need broad shoulders, thick skins and big feet to keep

us going!' I laughed. 'Anyway, what brings you here at this time of day?'

'It's our wedding anniversary, me and Elsie, nowt special, not gold or diamond or owt like that, but we're just having a bit of a celebration. Lunch out – that's a treat for us.'

'Well, I'd drink to your good health if I was allowed to have one while I'm on duty, but cheers anyway. Now, before you go, I think you can help me. I happened to hear you mention Witch Hill just a moment or two ago. I wasn't eavesdropping, mind, I just heard the words mentioned.'

'Aye, that's right. It was me! I was saying me and Doris had been to Witch Hill. Years ago, when we were courting.'

'So what is Witch Hill? I know where it is, I've been there in fact,but I don't know what it's got to do with courting couples.'

'Well, we go to Witch Hill when we start going steady, before we get engaged. I suppose it must be a way hereabouts of saying we're serious about each other. Making a commitment or summat, before we get engaged.'

'It's a long way from Aidensfield, I was up there recently and it's quite a distance from anywhere to be honest. I couldn't imagine courting couples walking all that way without some good reason.'

'Oh, we didn't actually go there, Mr Rhea, it's just a saying. When a lad and lass start going steady, they say they're going to Witch Hill. Then, after a while, they get engaged and then married. It's a way of saying they're promised to each other.'

'So you've never been to Witch Hill?'

'Not in the sense of physically going up there, no. To be honest with you, Mr Rhea, I'm not really sure where it is. I know it's up Gelderslack way somewhere on the moor but

I've never been. I say I went to Witch Hill because that was when me and Doris started going steady.'

'So the real Witch Hill has no actual part in a courtship?'

'Now I can't be sure about that, Mr Rhea. My dad and his dad before him and his dad before him allus said they went up to Witch Hill when they were courting and I think you'd find most of the older folks hereabouts, not just in Aidensfield either, allus reckoned they went up Witch Hill in their courting days.'

'It's a funny thing to say if Witch Hill hasn't any actual links with courtship,' I mused. 'There must be some reason why folks say that.'

'If there is, I can't tell you what it is, Mr Rhea, 'cos I've no idea . . . ah, Oscar. Drinks please, same again all round.'

And so my brief chat with Bob Cummings came to an end and when he returned to his table, I heard him raise the question with his wife and friends.

But no one seemed to know why local people used that strange expression. I left the pub no wiser about this odd saying, but with at least some of the customers trying to find the answer. The following weeks passed without me learning anything more about Witch Hill or its association with romance. Some time afterwards, Mary and I decided to go for a long countryside walk on the moors above Rannockdale. Mary's parents had offered to look after the children for the day – a Saturday – and so we embarked on our hike complete with rucksacks, hiking boots and waterproofs. The plan was to complete half the walk by around mid-day, have lunch at the Bluebell Inn in Rannockdale and finish our tour in time to return home for tea. By an odd coincidence – something I had not planned – the first half of our walk took us within sight of Witch Hill and so I found myself telling Mary all about its strange links with romance. But she could not suggest any reason for this, particularly as the hill was not especially prominent or scenic.

It was a fine and dry day in September and, on schedule, we arrived at the Bluebell Inn shortly after half-past twelve, ordered our drinks and lunch, and settled at one of the bar tables to enjoy it. Inevitably in these moorlands inns, there is always one or more of the village characters at the bar at lunch-time, and if strangers arrive it is likely the locals will try to engage them in conversation. In this instance, there was just one man in the bar, sitting on a high stool at the counter. As we sat with our drinks, awaiting our ham, egg and chips, the grizzly haired man at the bar, who clearly did not recognize me as a local policeman (and I did not recognize him either) called across,

'On holiday in these parts, are you?' He did not speak like a moorland resident; his accent was slightly refined although I could detect some local inflections. He looked to be of retiring age but was very casually dressed with a few days growth of grey beard. He looked as if he'd just come in from a session in his garden.

'Just a day out,' I said. 'Getting some fresh moorland air.'

'Been far then?'

'Up to the tops, over by Witch Hill and down here, then this afternoon we'll go down to the beck and back through the old abbey grounds. My car's in the car park there.'

'Witch Hill, eh? You're married then?'

'Oh yes, for several years now.'

'Then you'd no need to go to Witch Hill, had you?' and he laughed aloud. 'I once went up there with a girl, just after my parents came to live in these parts. I never knew about the tale behind Witch Hill so I had to marry her, hadn't I?'

'You actually went up to Witch Hill when you were courting?'

'Aye, but I wasn't really courting then, just going out with this lass. It wasn't serious, she wasn't my intended but she said mebbe I'd like to go for a walk up to Witch Hill. I thought it was a good idea so off we went, and when we got back, she said I had to marry her. I hadn't lived hereabouts for long then, my folks came over from Guisborough, and so I didn't know about Witch Hill at the time but it seemed any chap who went up there with a lass had to get married to her, her dad said that as well, so I married her.'

'You mean you were forced to marry her?'

'That's the way it looked to me. When I asked about it, I learned that taking a lass up Witch Hill was a feller's way of announcing his intentions. So without knowing it, I'd made it known I wanted to marry her. I didn't like to back out, well I couldn't really, being a man who honours his word and we're still married, I might add, and it's been good and happy so I've no regrets.'

I began to wonder if 'Going up Witch Hill' was some kind of code which indicated sexual relations or getting pregnant before marriage but did not suggest that.

'Why was that? Why was it a way of announcing you were going to marry her?' I asked as I replaced his pint of bitter with another, just to keep him talking. 'I knew there's some kind of link between Witch Hill and romance but I haven't been able to discover the whole story.'

'It took me a long time to find out,' he grinned. 'After I got wed, I began to wonder why going up Witch Hill meant I had to get wed to the woman I happened to be with at the time. It seemed a funny way of making a life-long commitment but she was a local lass who believed in all that stuff. And her dad did, he was very insistent. She was a nice lass, I might add, and still is. Then I discovered it's all to do with the bracken.'

'Bracken?' This was even more puzzling now!

'Aye, it grows on the moor around Witch Hill, lots of it, just below the tree line. Good strong bracken, acres of it.'

'I've seen it, it's thick and very deep.'

'Way back,' he said, taking a long draught of his beer. 'Way back, it was believed that if a man collected fern seeds he would become invisible or alternatively he could gain control over all living things. They believed that sort of thing in Europe an'all, not just here in England. I'm talking about the time we all believed in witches, sixteenth and seventeenth centuries or thereabouts. So if a young chap wasn't having any success in getting himself a wife, he would try and collect some fern seeds. If he managed to get them, it meant he could control the woman of his choice – and he could persuade her to marry him. That's what he honestly thought.'

'So all those unsuccessful and hopeful young men from hereabouts would go trekking up to Witch Hill to gather fern seeds because they'd got their eyes on a special young lady?'

'Right, young man. They weren't really seeds, of course, they were the spores of bracken, which is a type of fern, but it wasn't a simple task. It had to be done between eleven and midnight on Midsummer Eve. The youth had to go in total silence and lay a white cloth or a pewter dish on the ground under the bracken, and wait for the spores to fall. He mustn't shake the bracken or even touch it with his bare hands, although a forked hazel twig could be used to bend or direct the bracken stem in the hope the spores would fall on to the cloth when they were dislodged. But remember spores are extremely tiny and the smallest puff of wind would blow them away . . . and so gathering them was a most difficult task especially when witches were around in the darkness to make it even more difficult!'

I was beginning to see how this odd custom had started, even if it was now reduced to little more than a few words rather than actions.

'So once the lovesick youth had obtained his spores, he could then claim the girl of his dreams?'

'Right,' he said, taking another long draught from his glass, now almost empty. I bought him another, and then our food arrived, hot and steaming. 'I had unwittingly claimed my bride but because of that, everytime a couple began to go steady, it was said the lad was going to go to Witch Hill. In days gone by, that's exactly what love-sick lads did – on horseback or on foot – but now it's just a saying. In fact, it might mean something totally different now . . .'

And he grinned at his own salacious thoughts.

'Thanks for all that,' I said. 'You've solved a problem for me. I came across a man in Aidensfield a few weeks ago who told me a young couple would soon be going to Witch Hill. Now I know what he meant.'

'Do you really?' he grinned wickedly as we began to tuck into our tasty lunch.

Another tale of young love occurred when a girl from Aidensfield pursued a young man from Ashfordly, but the problem was that he did not love her nor indeed did he show the slightest interest in her. I think this one-sided romance had been kindled at secondary school, but any thoughts of them going to Witch Hill could not be contemplated, chiefly because the girl in question was only fifteen years old. Appropriately enough, her name was Juliet. Juliet Curtis.

The object of her devotion was much older – he was a

seventeen-year-old lad called Ian Brennan and although he worked as an apprentice for an Ashfordly butcher, his real passion was the theatre. This had been nurtured at secondary school where Ian had shown a talent which many thought would result in him becoming a full-time actor. Although there had been talk of him attending the Royal Academy of Dramatic Art (RADA), his parents insisted Ian qualified at some kind of trade or profession in case his dreams were not fulfilled. They pointed out that to earn one's living as an actor was both highly demanding and very insecure; only the best could hope to earn a decent living. And so, after leaving school at the age of sixteen, he worked in Rounton's Butcher's Shop in Ashfordly, a well-established family firm, learning how to slaughter animals, cut their meat and display it for sale. By the time he reached twenty-one, he would be a qualified butcher, his parents believing that with such a qualification he would never be out of work. At that stage, he would be an adult, so he could then make up his own mind about any other career.

Due to his keen interest in the theatre, however, he spent all his spare time travelling to stage productions in the region, sometimes even riding his bike and later his motor bike to attend them; he went to theatres in Newcastle, Sunderland, Darlington, Middlesbrough, York, Scarborough, Whitby, Hull, Leeds, Sheffield and even London to observe and learn about his desired profession. In his holidays, he sometimes obtained work back stage, helping with the scenery, sound or lighting or even just making the tea – anything to keep him in touch with the theatre.

If there was any hint of an amateur production or a pantomime within striking distance of home, he would audition for a part – and he often succeeded. With all those commitments outside his work, it meant he was usually away from Ashfordly when not working in the shop. As he was away most evenings and weekends, the only time Juliet could contrive to snatch a word with him, or even a merest glimpse, was when she went shopping in Ashfordly with her mother. She would insist she wanted a pork pie and some sausages from Rounton's, always making some excuse to visit the shop. Quite often, she was disappointed because Ian would be working behind the scenes, perhaps in the slaughter house, but she never gave up. She was determined to secure Ian Brennan as her special boy friend and was prepared to go to almost any lengths to win his interest and affection.

One of her frustrations was the close parental supervision she had to endure, especially as she lived in Aidensfield which was four or five miles from Ashfordly. It meant that when Ian went off to watch or take part in a production some distance from home, often spending time away in theatrical lodgings, she could not go with him; her only possible opportunities to snatch a few moments with him were when he was behind the counter in the shop in Ashfordly. However, there were a few other occasions when she could attempt to assail him in the street while she was out of school; after all, he did deliver meat from a butcher's bike and so, from time to time, she was able to ambush him having learned his usual delivery route – school bus times permitting of course.

As the village constable of Aidensfield, and with regular patrol duties in Ashfordly, I became aware of this rather one-sided romance and felt some admiration for Juliet in persisting with her unrequited ardour. She was a likeable youngster, bubbly and attractive and apparently undaunted by Ian's lack of response. In fact, his reticence served only to make her more determined. She was a short girl, only about five feet tall and rather plump with mousey hair, and she appeared to have no deep interests other than her passion for Ian.

I later discovered she was quite good at school sports such as hockey and netball but no doubt like many other people in Aidensfield, I began to wonder how Juliet's pursuit of Ian would conclude. Dominated his own determination to follow a theatrical career, he seemed blissfully unaware of her passion. There was little doubt he thought of nothing but life within the theatrical environment. I guessed that once he achieved that ambition, true love might follow.

Those of us who knew Ian liked him. He was a tall, slender youth with a shock of dark, curly hair and a handsome face with laughing dark eyes. He moved with a casual grace and oozed confidence in everything he did; he'd been very good at athletics while at school, throwing the javelin being one of his special skills. He was not keen on contact sports like soccer or rugby football but seemed to excel in those requiring graceful strength, such as throwing the javelin, running the hundred yards and even bowling at cricket. Although he'd enjoyed those sports at school, he did not seem anxious to continue them once he'd left and his lack of interest in Juliet, and girls in general, prompted some to wonder about his sexual orientation.

So far as I was aware, however, there was never any hint of a homosexual aspect to his life; if there was, he managed to keep it hidden.

For all Juliet's devotion to him, it never seemed to occur to her that she might find a way to his heart by also showing an open interest in things theatrical. I suspect she regarded the theatre as a competitor for his affections whereas she might have used it as a means of attracting him. In fact, of course, her isolation in Aidensfield made it very difficult for her to go to the theatre, even in a nearby town, for she had no transport of her own, apart from an old pedal cycle. Those of us who knew her realized how difficult it was for her to travel away with Ian or even to attend a show as a member of the audience. There were occasions when theatrical events were staged within fairly easy reach of Ashfordly or Aidensfield, and they included the theatres in Scarborough, Whitby Spa and York. So why did she not persuade her parents to take her to some of those performances?

The truth was that Juliet's one-sided affair with Ian was nothing to do with anyone else but as the Aidensfield village constable I considered it part of my duty to know everything that was happening around me, even things which may not be related to crime and criminals. It must also be said that Juliet's activities did create interest in most of the residents. Most of us wondered how it would end – after all, there were nearly four more years before Ian reached the magic age of 21 and spread his wings over a wider patch of England. We felt that if she wanted him for herself, she must catch him before he left Ashfordly on his quest for greater theatrical satisfaction.

Then things took a fascinating turn and I felt pleased to be part of those events at their earliest stage. It was an early spring day and I was patrolling Ashfordly because there was a shortage of local constables due to one being on annual leave, another attending court with a careless driving case and a third on a refresher course. And it was the Sergeant's rest day, the first of his three-day weekend. Only Alf Ventress remained and he was due to work a late turn in the town, i.e. 2 p.m. until 10 p.m. I was therefore filling the gap between 9 a.m. and 2 p.m. chiefly because it was a Friday, market day, when the town would be busy. That was always an enjoyable duty because the bustle and banter of the market with its stallholders and customers was both entertaining and interesting.

It was around half past twelve and I was standing on the higher steps of the huge memorial to the third Baron Ashfordly, gazing across the colourful scene below me, when a man climbed towards me and stood at my side. He was around forty years old, I guessed, a tall, well-built character whose clothing set him apart from the country people who thronged the market. He wore a green corduroy jacket, a yellow neckband and faded blue jeans over deep purple shoes. His dark, well-kept hair was rather longer than a local man would wear it but that was now fashionable due to the impact of the Beatles.

'Splendid rural atmosphere, constable,' he said in a very cultured accent, smiling in pleasure at the picture-postcard scene below us. We could see the canvas roofs of the stalls and the queues at each; we could hear the chatter rising from the market and smell food being cooked somewhere.

Music was playing too while cars and people seemed constantly on the move.

'Lovely,' I said. 'And I call this work!'

'I'm sure it's not always like this, but enjoy it while you can. Now, constable, I wonder if you can help me.'

One of the regular tasks of a constable in a tourist area like Ashfordly was to answer questions from visitors. They might ask about anything from where to obtain a nice meal or bed-and-breakfast to the history of the local castle or abbey. At times, we felt as if we were walking encyclopedias. Clearly, this man was a visitor; his accent and mode of dress told me that.

'I'll do my best.'

'Would you know who owns the castle?' and he pointed to the ruin whose walls towered above the town. They could be seen from almost every part of Ashfordly and from all the approach roads.

'It belongs to Ashfordly Estate,' I could answer that with ease. 'Lord Ashfordly is the head of the family, and he owns most of the buildings you can see around us, including the market place itself.'

'All very feudal?' he grinned mischievously.

'In the opinion of some, yes, but he stops a lot of silly and unsightly attempts at developing the town,' I responded. 'And he's generous towards the townspeople and his tenants. We've no complaints. You can see how successful the system is by just looking around you. There's no inner city deterioration and grime here! That's why we get so many people coming to enjoy Ashfordly.'

'That's what I like to hear, constable. Pride in your surroundings. So do you think he would lend me his castle?'

'Lend it to you?'

'Yes, lend it to me. Is it open to the public?'

'Yes, on a fairly regular basis. During the summer season mostly, to cater for tourists. From ten until five every day between Easter Sunday and the last Sunday in September. And he does allow the occasional event inside the grounds or even within the castle walls, that's at any time of the year. Garden fêtes, a concert by the local brass band, charity fund-raising parties, even a show of classic cars, that sort of thing.'

'This sounds promising, constable. So where do I find the estate office? I'd like a look around the castle while I'm here . . .'

'It is closed at the moment,' I felt I had to warn him. 'But if you've a special interest, I'm sure the estate staff will show you round. It's a ruin as you can see from here although some of its buildings have been roofed. One of them contains a small museum. If you want to ask, the estate office is behind Ashfordly Hall, you'll see the direction signs when you go through those gates just beyond the market place, they take you into the grounds of the Hall,' and I indicated the direction.

'It sounds perfect for my needs,' he smiled. 'Now tell me this, has a play ever been staged in the grounds? In the open air?'

'Not to my knowledge, but I've only been in the district for a few years,' I admitted. 'I think if one had been staged recently, I'd have known about it.'

'That's what I want to do, constable. I want to present Shakespeare in a setting which is as close as possible to the period and the background about which he wrote. In many ways, a medieval castle is ideal. My plan is to stage this kind of show in castles and abbeys around Britain, but not by using professional actors. I want to use young people, school children perhaps, and it would be a wonderful means of getting them – and their parents – to understand and appreciate Shakespeare.'

'Our local secondary schools are very good at that kind of thing,' I said. 'We've a very progressive secondary modern school at Seavham, that's between here and Brantsford, and a very successful grammar school here in Ashfordly. Both put on excellent performances, and I'd suggest you contact them too. You'd find them most co-operative,' and I told him where to find the schools.

'I'd like to use the children but we might need someone with a bit of experience to play the leading parts, they have to carry the entire performance.'

He chatted for a further few minutes about his plans, saying he hoped to produce Romeo and Juliet in Ashfordly Castle and adding that he was a professional freelance producer of stage plays. He told me his name was Barnaby Mayer and he could be contacted through the office at the Royal Shakespeare Theatre at Stratford-on-Avon; the staff would pass along any messages or mail. Then I decided to tell him about Ian Brennan. He seemed very keen to make use of the best of local talent, not only in the acting side of his production but also in administrative work and back-stage.

I told him where to find Ian and he said he would pay him a visit. Thanking me for my help, he stepped down from the memorial and disappeared among the crowd. I returned to more mundane things, with a lady approaching me to say she'd lost her purse. That brought me gently back to routine police work.

I thought no more about my chat with Barnaby Mayer until some days later when I was in the post office at Aidensfield. It was a Saturday morning and there was a small queue of four people. I awaited my turn to buy a postal order and realized the person immediately in front of me was Juliet Curtis. Seeing her reminded me of Ian Brennan which in turn reminded me of that chat with Barnaby Mayer.

'Hello, Juliet,' I greeted her. 'How's things?'

'Fine, Mr Rhea, thank you. I'm just getting some stamps for mum, she wants to send a parcel to Aunt Celia, it's her birthday next week.'

'I'm ordering some records from a catalogue,' I told her. 'I need a postal order. That's the penalty of living in such a quiet place, everything has to be done from afar! So how's school?'

'Fine, we're working for our mock O-levels, there's a lot to do.'

'I was talking to a man the other day, I told him to get in touch with your school because he's thinking of putting on a play in the grounds of Ashfordly Castle, I told him the local schools put on some very good plays.'

'He's already been, Mr Rhea, it was announced at assembly a few days ago. He wants to involve as many of us as possible, from both schools, he said he'd got permission to stage the play in the castle. It sounds very exciting.'

'I told him about Ian Brennan,' I wondered if my ploy sounded too outrageously obvious. 'He said it might be necessary to use experienced people for the lead roles. He was talking about doing *Romeo and Juliet*.'

'It is, Mr Rhea, that's the one he's going to put on, our teachers are having a meeting about it, to see who's going to take the parts and do the back-stage work and so on. I think Ian's name was mentioned as Romeo.'

'Then you should be Juliet!' I heard myself say. 'I think you'd produce a wonderful Juliet.'

'Oh, no, Mr Rhea, I couldn't, I've never done anything like that, they've never picked me for a school play, not ever, besides, Juliet was old enough to get married and I'm too young . . .'

'Juliet was only fourteen,' I reminded her. 'In fact, I don't think she was as old as that.'

She didn't answer but I felt I had given her something to think about. During those moments of silence as the queue moved forward, I could imagine this Juliet in the role of her namesake because she would not be acting a part, she'd be playing herself. If only she could produce her own deepest emotions in a manner which was in keeping with that famous role, she'd deliver a memorable performance. Or so I thought. I heard nothing more of that plan until I read an item in the local *Gazette* which announced that Ashfordly Castle was going to be the autumn venue of a special production of *Romeo and Juliet*, with local schoolchildren and young people playing all the roles.

Ian Brennan was to play Romeo and I was amazed and delighted that Juliet was going to play her namesake. It must have taken some courage on her part to audition for the role and I felt it was her love for Ian which had enabled her to convince the selectors that she was right for the part.

There is nothing much more I can add to this story except that Mary, the children and I went along to the performance in its stunning setting and Juliet, with all the emotion that a love-sick girl had to deliver, produced a magnificent and moving portrayal of the other Juliet. I knew, and I think everyone in the audience knew, she was being herself even if the words spoken were from the Bard himself.

After the performance, I saw Ian and Juliet walking in the castle grounds, hand in hand.

I must admit I began to wonder how long it would be before they went up Witch Hill.

Chapter 8

Among the problems experienced by police officers is the reliability or otherwise of eye-witnesses. Such people are vital to the processes of law and order when they observe something like a crime being committed or a road traffic accident actually happening or even someone behaving suspiciously. The snag is that so many witnesses are unreliable, not because they are untruthful but because they honestly believe that what they have seen is the true version of events. It is unfortunate that on occasions an eye-witness can be wrong which in turn means their interpretation of an incident can be misleading or even dangerous.

With this in mind, our Chief Constable arranged a day's training for twenty newly appointed magistrates. It would be dedicated to the skills of observation because the Government thought it necessary that these administrators of local justice should be aware of such pitfalls. The course, which was at our local police training school, comprised a series of lectures and practical demonstrations. After coffee, one of the first exercises was to assemble on the parking area in front of the main building to view the landscape spread across the dale below. They had to look at it for a mere ten seconds then write a short report on what they noticed within that time. It was a simple exercise to see which features dominated and why; some magistrates might, for example, refer only to the herd of cows in the nearby field, others might mention the range of hills in the background while others may concentrate on the main road in the far distance or the grand houses in the near distance. Some might even notice the main London–Edinburgh railway line.

With twenty magistrates, it was felt that twenty different descriptions of the same view would result. Later in the day, there would be a discussion about those differences and it was hoped this would alert the students to the dangers of placing too much reliance upon what a single witness claimed to have noticed in a split second. For the exercise, they would all have to stand with their backs to the view, and then turn around and back again at a given command. In those few seconds while they were gazing across the landscape, an open-topped bright red sports car hurtled along the lane just below them. Only yards away at the end of the training school's own drive, it was driven by a man who wore a bright yellow scarf around his neck; it was stretched out behind him in the slipstream, then the car slowed down with a screech of brakes and swung right with a squealing of tyres into the private road leading to a country house. It then accelerated noisily towards the house and vanished behind some outbuildings.

'Did you see that?' the police instructor asked, and they all nodded whereupon he said, 'Then include it in your report. Remember, if you were police officers, you would have to identify that driver – and the car – if he was to be prosecuted in court.'

In the classroom later that day, each of them referred to the high speed of the red sports car and the reckless behaviour of its driver but none had noticed its registration number. They had noticed, however, that the driver wore a bright yellow scarf. After lunch, a red sports car eased to a halt outside the front door, on the very car park used as their observation platform, and it was escorted by a police car driven by a traffic patrol officer.

Sitting in their classroom, the magistrates could observe this arrival and after a few moments, the traffic officer came into the classroom accompanied by a young man wearing a brown leather coat and a long yellow scarf. In solemn terms, the constable described how he had received a complaint about the dangerous driving of the sports car, saying he had traced it and its driver; the person who had called the police had noticed the students standing outside the training school on its elevated site, and had suggested they might have witnessed the event. When the policeman asked if anyone had seen the incident, most showed their hands although a few withheld such a commitment, and then he asked if the man standing beside him was the driver. Most of them nodded or murmured their agreement.

'But he's not the driver,' smiled the traffic constable. 'That incident was an exercise we created deliberately to see how you would react as witnesses. I think you all saw the car, you noticed it was red, that it was a sports car, that it was driven by a man and the method of driving left a lot to be desired. I know none of you obtained its registration number which means the car outside might not be the actual vehicle involved – that's a point to remember – but in any case, this man was not the driver. You identified the yellow scarf, not the man who was wearing it.'

It was a simple but effective means of highlighting the vulnerability of eyewitnesses and this kind of test has been used many times during training sessions, in similar but differing guises. That modest test came to mind some years later when I received an urgent telephone call from a motorist.

I must admit that, at the time, I did not recollect our demonstration to the magistrates – that memory came later – but a very similar lesson was learned, with a most curious outcome.

I was performing night duty from 10 p.m. until 6 a.m., patrolling the section based on Ashfordly and Brantsford. I was using the section car, a Ford Anglia. These duties came around every three months or so, with all the constables in the section taking their turn and although none of us relished night shift, it did enable us to visit villages and locations we might otherwise never see. Sometimes we had incidents to occupy us, such as traffic accidents, outbreaks of fire, reports of suspicious behaviour, complaints of late night noise at pubs or house parties, or specific observations on particular premises. There were occasions, of course, when nothing happened so we spent all night driving around and checking vulnerable property, wondering how best to otherwise occupy ourselves. In all cases, though, we had a mid-shift break starting around 1.30 a.m. which we took at either Ashfordly or Brantsford Police Station. There, with a nice coal fire during the winter months, we could enjoy our sandwiches and flask of coffee or tea but even though that forty-five minutes was our official break time, it meant we were also liable to be contacted if required, and also duty-bound to deal with any matter that arose.

While settling down to enjoy my sandwiches one fine but

cool night in October, the telephone rang. Sighing with slight frustration at my meal being interrupted almost before I had started, I heard coins drop into a box and button 'A' being pressed; this told me the call was coming from a kiosk.

'Ashfordly Police, PC Rhea speaking,' I announced.

'Ah, police, good, can you come quickly. There's a woman running about in the woods, she looks extremely distressed. I think she needs help.'

Knowing that the caller's money might soon run out, I had to be brief, so I asked, 'Where?'

'The woods at Crampton Bank Top.'

'I'll come straight away, it'll take me twenty minutes. Can you wait and tell me more when I get there?'

'Sure, no problem. There's eight of us, we'll keep looking for her but I thought you should know, in case she's on the run from somewhere.'

'You could be right. And your name?'

'Conway, Frank Conway from Thirsk.'

'See you in twenty minutes, Mr Conway.'

I rang our Sub-Divisional office at Eltering to say I'd be away from the office investigating the report of a distressed woman running about in Crampton Woods and apparently in need of help. I then asked whether there had been any reports of women missing from home, absent from any institution or perhaps fleeing from a hospital. I knew there was none in the Ashfordly district but Eltering covered a wider area, yet I was assured there had been no such reports. The duty constable, John Rogers, asked whether I required assistance to mount a co-ordinated search but at that early stage, I declined, saying I must assess the situation before deciding on a further course of action.

I promised a situation report as soon as possible, adding I would be on the air in the section car if he needed to contact me. It was feasible a report of such a woman might be received while I was on the road. I re-packed my sandwiches and flask in the hope I'd be able to snatch a bite or two and departed for Crampton Bank Top. There were a couple of private hospitals and half a dozen old folks' homes in some nearby villages, so it was possible that a patient could have wandered off and somehow got into those woods, in spite of the fact that Crampton Bank Top was rather isolated.

It was also possible that if a woman had fled from an institution of some kind, or even run away from her private home, her absence might not yet have been noticed and no alarm raised. As I drove the few miles, I pondered the situation and wondered if there really was a problem or whether the sighting was nothing more than a woman getting some fresh air because she couldn't sleep. But I was duty bound to investigate the report.

Crampton Rigg ran almost directly west to east from the edge of Aidensfield towards Crampton, a distance of about three miles, while rising to about eight hundred feet above sea level. From its heights, there were spectacular views to the north and south. Its northern face sloped gently down to the river about a mile away while its southern aspect was much steeper, being more like a cliff face with crags and high vertical rocks. Not surprisingly, it was a popular location for walks and horse-riding with a bridleway running along the ridge and more public paths in the woods.

Several parts of the ridge, including that part which crossed Crampton Bank Top, were covered with mature trees, both coniferous and deciduous but at that point the road from Crampton effectively divided the woodland into two long and narrow stretches. Once it crossed the summit, the road, there known as Crampton Bank, dropped steeply down to the plain below but on the summit there were seats, a parking area, a telephone kiosk and observation point. During the summer it was always popular with tourists and locals alike because of the extensive views and on balmy summer evenings, it was frequented by courting couples. As I motored through the pretty countryside, I wondered if Mr Conway's sighting had been a woman visiting this popular place for reasons best known to herself, although it was a strange time of day to do so.

When I arrived, I saw two cars on the parking area, each showing their sidelights, and I eased to a halt beside them. It was almost two o'clock in the morning, fine and dry with no moon, and I could see a small crowd of people waiting to talk to me. Some were carrying torches and as I eased to a halt, one of the men approached as the others gathered round.

'I'm Frank Conway,' he was in his late fifties, I estimated, and dressed in a smart dark suit. 'It was me who rang.'

'PC Rhea,' I introduced myself. 'I'm the village bobby at Aidensfield and this is part of my patch but I'm working from Ashfordly tonight. So, any more sightings of the woman?'

'No,' they all muttered and shook their heads, and I noticed they were all smartly dressed, and all in their early fifties. Four men and four women, husbands and wives by the look of things. I wondered where they had been and how they had come to be together at this time of night in such a lonely place; I could not smell any alcohol on their breath and they were most certainly not in a frivolous mood. In fact, they were just the opposite – they looked stone-cold-sober and very concerned about the mystery woman.

Frank Conway explained that after calling me they had split into two groups of four, each group armed with torches. Each group, comprising husbands and wives, had walked along the bridleway to cover around three quarters of a mile in either direction. None had found any sign of the mystery woman in spite of searching with their torches and calling out for some kind of response. At times they had stood in silence, listening for her movements or sounds of distressed breathing, but they had heard nothing. It was if she had vanished into thin air.

'These cars?' I indicated. 'Are they both yours?'

'Yes, we're together, two car loads. We looked for another car or a bike, but there's none. She must have walked from somewhere to get here. The village isn't far away.'

I explained that I had checked with my Sub-Divisional Headquarters but there had been no recent reports of a missing woman but decided to make another check before taking further action. I radioed John Rogers at Eltering to report my arrival at Crampton Bank Top and he confirmed his previous statement.

There were no reports of women currently missing in this locality and so I told him I would carry out a brief search and call him in due course.

'So whoever she was and whatever her reason for being here, there's no sign of her now?' I put to them all.

'No, we've not seen or heard her, she's not come back. I can't understand it,' one of the women said. 'We all saw her, she was definitely upset or distressed about something and she ran across the road from that side,' and she pointed to the east where the bridlepath joined the main highway, 'then she went across to that other side, and vanished along the bridleway, into those trees. We all stopped straight away, only moments behind her and went to see if she needed help, but she'd vanished.'

'And you all saw her?'

They murmured their positive responses and so I asked Conway, 'Can you describe her?'

'Average height,' he began. 'Five foot five or six, I'd say, about thirty six or seven years old, slim with long dark hair and wearing strange clothes, very old fashioned, a long dark dress, black I think or some very dark colour like green with long sleeves and a high neck. No hat, no ribbons in her hair. She was running with one hand to her head, her left hand, as if crying or upset or frightened. Terrified even. We all saw her, two car loads of us, we were coming up the hill when she ran across the road right in our headlights, as clear as anything. I was driving the first car so I pulled into this parking area and got out to see if she needed help, but she'd gone.'

'She couldn't have gone far, we stopped only seconds after seeing her,' added one of the women.

The description was rather too vague to match anyone I knew to be living in Crampton or its neighbouring villages. 'Did you see anyone else?' I asked. 'Was anyone chasing her?'

'No, we've not seen anyone else. She was quite alone, I can guarantee that. I'm sure she wasn't being chased, or that she wasn't chasing anyone or anything such as a dog.'

'Was she carrying anything? Rucksack? Handbag? Bag of any kind?'

'No, nothing. Not even a torch, even though it was dark.'

'It's all very odd, I agree. So how long do you think it was between seeing her and getting out to try and help? Can you be precise about this?'

'It can't have been long, Mr Rhea. Half a minute maybe. Less even. I shone my torch along that bridleway, the way she went, but there was no sign of her, so we all decided to check along both sides but there was nothing. No sound or sight of her. It was just as if she had vanished into thin air, that's when we decided to call you.'

'Without any report of a vulnerable woman being missing, there's not a great deal I can do,' I had to tell them. 'I appreciate your concern but if she's an adult she's quite entitled to run around these woods in the early hours of the morning if she wants to. These woods are riddled with public paths, she could be anywhere. If she is a fitness fanatic, she could be back at home now, tucked safely in bed somewhere in Crampton while we're out here worrying about her.'

'I appreciate that. I rang in case you knew of anyone who's absent or missing without reason,' Conway said. 'I don't expect you to mount a massive search party for something like this, but I thought it should be reported, as a precaution, just in case she has run away from somewhere and is vulnerable. Certainly, she looked highly distressed, that's why I rang you.'

'You did absolutely the right thing and I appreciate your concern,' I said. 'Before I leave, I'll have a walk along that bridleway myself, just to make sure she's not lying injured or hiding somewhere. I'll go without a torch and will put my car lights out; I know the route well enough and will rely on my ears! If she is hiding from us, that might reveal her whereabouts.'

'Thanks, it's good to know something is being done, we are all very concerned.'

'So my next question is – what on earth brings you all here at this time of the morning?'

'We've been to an evening service in Lincoln Cathedral, a commemorative one for members of our regiment, wives and husbands from all over. It's a sort of re-union after the war. Then tonight we had to wait for the ferry back across the Humber which made things late and that's it, we're all on our way home.'

'Thanks, well, just before you leave, I'll check again with our office to make sure no one's reported missing.'

Once again, I checked with John Rogers at Eltering and he reaffirmed that no women had been reported missing, then said, 'Hang on, Nick, the sergeant's just come in.'

He handed the phone to the night duty sergeant who'd just returned from supervising some of his own night shift, so that I could explain things to him. After hearing my account, Sergeant Young advised that no formal search should be undertaken on the grounds that the woman, an adult, did not appear to be missing, or being chased by anyone or in need of any kind of assistance. It seemed, he said, that she was doing nothing more than taking a late night run in the woods for reasons best known to herself, her peculiar attire probably being her nightdress. He told me to make a comprehensive entry in the Occurrence Book at Ashfordly Police Station and he would do likewise at Eltering, just in case a Missing Person Report was later received. And he had no objection to me making a final search of the woodland, just to satisfy myself she was not lying injured or distressed in some quiet place. I assured him and the witnesses that I would return in daylight to make another search, and would also make enquiries in the locality in the hope that someone recognised the mystery woman.

Frank Conway heard all these exchanges over the police radio and expressed his satisfaction. I thanked him for his public spirited reaction and took his personal details, including his telephone number, so that I could update him on any further progress. He thanked me and said he understood that no further action could sensibly be taken, and so he and his friends departed for home.

I sat in my police car for a few minutes to finish my sandwiches and flask for I was very hungry, then made my final search along almost a mile of the bridleway and into the bordering woodland.

I found no sign of anyone and even though I spent some time in utter darkness among the trees, just listening for sounds of movement, I heard nothing. I returned to Ashfordly Police Station to write up a very detailed account in the Occurrence Book and then set about completing the final part of my night shift.

It would be a couple of days later, when I had returned to late shifts (2 p.m. until 10 p.m.), that I was in Ashfordly Police Station once again. I knew there had been no further developments in the search for the distressed woman; none had been reported missing in the district and my own daylight search of the bridleway at Crampton Bank Top had proved fruitless. Furthermore, I had been unable to identify the woman as anyone living locally in spite of enquiries in the locality. But when I walked into the station shortly after 3 p.m. to deliver some reports, I found Alf Ventress on duty at the desk. He had been away, enjoying a fishing trip on his two weekly rest days, and had now returned to duty. For the first time, therefore, he had seen my report about the woman at Crampton Bank Top.

'That woman at Crampton Bank Top,' he smiled wickedly. 'You know who it is, don't you?'

'I wish I did!'

'Abigail Crowther,' he beamed mischievously.

'Should I know her?' I asked in all innocence.

'You should, being the Aidensfield bobby, but clearly you don't, Nick. She used to live in Crampton.'

'So where does she live now?' I could see I was having to drag this information from him.

'She doesn't, she died. More than three hundred and fifty years ago. She was suspected of being a witch, Nick, and the villagers chased her to the top of one of those cliffs near Crampton Bank Top. They were going to hang her so she ran for her life but tripped and fell down the cliff face. She was killed in the fall, Nick. Her ghost is regularly seen there, we get reports every so often, always sightings of a very distressed dark haired woman in a long dress running as if fleeing for her life. Those who see her think she's a real person, like those people of yours did. I can't remember any time when eight folks saw her all at once, though, so that must be some kind of record. Anyway, that's who they saw. Abigail Crowther.'

'I don't believe it, Alf!'

'Then check with the library, Nick.'

I did. I found a book which listed local hauntings and it contained the sad story of Abigail Crowther, with lots of recorded sightings to match the one given to me on that occasion. The book also recorded a similar tale linked to Sutton Bank Top, one also generating regular sightings of a ghost. I decided to ring Frank Conway at Thirsk to give him this piece of news but I didn't tell him Abigail was a ghost – I said we had identified the mystery woman as a local person called Abigail Crowther and then told him about the book so that he could read the account and so make up his own mind.

I never heard from him again.

So had he and his friends really seen the ghost of Abigail Crowther? Or was it merely a real live local woman running in the woods at night? We may never know.

Another difficulty for a police officer so far as eye-witnesses are concerned is obtaining a truly accurate description of a criminal suspect. If a witness catches only a fleeting glimpse, this is quite understandable and it is equally understandable when the only witness is the victim of the crime. Victims are often severly traumatized by the experience. One can fully appreciate, say, the victim of a rape or violent assault being unable to describe their assailant in detail, and there are similar difficulties where old people are victims or mere witnesses. Abstracting a viable description is sometimes impossible, certainly insufficient to justify an arrest and therefore inadequate for prosecution purposes.

Another difficulty is often due to the perception of the witness. For example, suppose a forty year old thief rushed into a shop, grabbed a fistful of money from the till and absconded down the street. The shop assistant, perhaps one or more customers and even some people in the street might see him, but would they provide the same description? If one of the witnesses was a teenager, he might say the thief was a middle aged man; a pensioner seeing the same villain might describe him as a young man while someone of the same age might regard him as either being younger or older than himself.

If the thief was, say, five feet eight inches tall, a woman who was five feet two inches tall might say he was a tall young man while a six-foot man would consider him to be rather small. It all depends upon how a witness views things and it is the police officer's task to abstract the correct information. I recall one witness who described a man as wearing a brown jacket when in fact the jacket was green; it transpired the witness was partially colour-blind so far as certain shades of brown and green were concerned. I can also recall an 80-year old woman who witnessed a bad case of dangerous driving and described the offender as a stupid young man. When we traced him, he was fifty-five years old.

When interviewing witnesses, therefore, experienced police officers will always gently press the witness for more necessary detail. He will not accept 'tall' and 'short' as sufficient description of a person's height, always trying to obtain some better indication, even comparing such heights with the witness's own stature. The same applies to age. 'Young', 'old' or 'middle-aged' are not precise enough and so attempts are made to indicate an age, even an approximate one. It's always useful if a witness says, 'Oh, he was five or six years older/younger than me.' I've even spoken to witnesses who were unsure whether the person they saw was male or female, black or white, old or young. The phrase 'Oh, he was just an an ordinary sort of man' could fit millions of people in this country. What the police need is much more detail, if possible with some other striking feature such as a beard, moustache, spectacles, one leg missing, dark skin, a limp, gold rings on her fingers and even bells on her toes.

It follows that a positive identification is highly important and the finest method is a street identification. That is where a witness happens to catch sight of a suspect in a street or public place; this occurs from time to time. In one case in Ashfordly, a woman had her handbag snatched by a youth who ran off and two weeks later, she saw him walking down the street and recognized him. If such a witness can either name the suspect, follow him or her to some home address or call a police officer before the suspect disappears, then this spontaneous evidence is always regarded as valuable. The next best thing is the identification parade.

This method is by no means perfect and far from ideal, but it can and does help to identify a criminal. It was not widely used during my time as the constable at Aidensfield because it was often regarded as a kind of last resort, but it was something we would use if circumstances demanded. The system sounded fairly simple. If the question of a suspect's identity was in doubt, and if it was thought a witness could point to the suspect when confronted by him or her, the police would stage an identification parade. This entailed a line-up of at least eight people, one of whom was the suspect. The others had to be similar to the suspect in appearance, age and dress, so if the suspect had a broken left leg, then the police had to find others with a like injury. Alternatively they might conceal his infirmity behind something like a counter which meant the other seven did not need to suffer from a broken left leg in order to take part. It was not easy finding several men with handlebar moustaches, limps, glass eyes, smelly breath, spotty complexions, larger than normal feet, white pigtails or some other feature adopted by the suspect.

But it was good fun trying to persuade people to volunteer to take part, their chief worry being that they might be selected as the villain! There were certain safeguards, however. First, the suspect had to agree to the parade, and if he or she did agree, then it was permissible to have a friend or solicitor present. Photographs of the suspect must not be shown to the witnesses beforehand, nor must the suspect or members of the line-up be seen by any of the witnesses prior to the parade. The suspect must be allowed to stand anywhere he wished in the line-up, and if there were several witnesses, he could change places after each one had completed his viewing.

Police officers could not be used in the line-up and one of the more difficult tasks was for the witnesses to actually touch the person they identified. This was done by placing a hand on the shoulder and was done to eliminate doubt – if they merely pointed to the person, there might be a suggestion that the wrong person had been indicated. Sometimes, if the case was one of rape or violence, they were allowed to touch the selected person from the rear so they did not have to face their assailant. If a witness asked for the suspect to do some act, like walk or shake his head, or put on a hat or scarf, or speak some particular words, then everyone in the line-up must do likewise. Normally, there were no observers at the parade, other than senior officers and the police officer in charge of the case; a second officer involved in the case might also be there to provide corroborative evidence. It was possible, however, for other police officers to be present for training purposes but this had to receive the approval of the suspect.

Every facet of the parade must be carefully recorded and the prisoner had to be asked whether it had been conducted to his satisfaction. There must not be the slightest suggestion that witnesses had been influenced in their choice and the suspect was always advised to object if there was any aspect, however minor, which he considered unsatisfactory.

The recruitment of volunteers was never easy. Quite often, it meant a tour of the local pubs, clubs and dole offices to see whether any of the characters there might like to help – and the bribe was a fee. Everyone who took part was paid half-a-crown (2s.6d – 12.5p) for their time. In the 1960s, that would buy them a couple of pints of beer, considered by some to be a just reward.

When Miss Ada Potter aged 76, a spinster of the parish of Ashfordly, was knocked to the ground by a young villain who legged it with her handbag and contents, it was decided to hold an identification parade because the physical description of her attacker matched a local youth called Wayne Waters. Wayne was an up-and-coming nuisance, a stupid youth aged 17 who thought he was being funny by smashing shop windows, stealing handbags from unsuspecting women, trampling over people's gardens and flower beds, breaking radio aerials on cars, letting down tyres of buses left outside overnight, chalking graffiti on walls and swearing at clergymen. He was also a known shoplifter whose speciality was sweets and bars of chocolate and he had even been suspected of grabbing apples and pears from displays outside the local fruit shop. He had been caught on occasions and dealt with by the juvenile court but it seemed he was determined to continue his career as a pest.

In the case of Miss Potter, a rather fragile lady, she had been shopping in the market place at Ashfordly and was heading for the bus stop with a heavy bag of groceries in one hand and her handbag in the other. Wayne had galloped towards her with the appearance of hurrying to catch a bus but as he'd reached her, he'd shouted something, pushed her to the ground and grabbed the handle of her handbag to snatch it from her grasp before running off to leave her screaming for the police. The spirited Miss Potter made enough din to jerk even the most lethargic of shoppers into action but in the subsequent confusion, the robber escaped. The bag had been found later in someone's garden, minus the cash; it had only contained six pounds ten shillings, but that was a lot of money for a lady of very modest means.

Miss Potter could not provide a very clear description of her assailant even though she had seen his full face – but she did say she felt sure she would recognize him again if she saw him face to face. Thanks to some rapid police work, several witnesses were traced who were able to provide a more detailed description of the fleeing villain; it could only match Wayne Waters. Their descriptions said he was a young man in his teens, about seventeen or eighteen, slim build with long black hair which was quite curly and piled up on top. He had long sideburns and was wearing pale blue jeans, a black leather jacket, a pink shirt and bright purple shoes with thick silent soles. That was Wayne's version of a teddy boy outfit and, at that time, he was one of very few lads in Ashfordly to wear such distinctive clothes. We knew our man.

Because this crime was classified as robbery, the CID were called in to investigate it and it was inevitable that Wayne was arrested and questioned.

True to form, he denied being responsible and insisted he had not been anywhere near the market place in Ashfordly that day. The officer in charge of the enquiry, Detective

Sergeant Howard Bedford from Eltering, had interviewed the other witnesses and without exception they provided a description which matched that of Wayne. It looked a clear case against him but in spite of the evidence and despite being held in custody overnight, Wayne persisted in his denials. Because Miss Potter had claimed she would recognise her attacker if she saw him face to face, Detective Sergeant Bedford, a smart 45-year old who always dressed impeccably, decided to hold an identification parade at which Ada would be requested to pick out her assailant. Due to a lack of space in Ashfordly police station, it was decided to hold the parade in the court house where there was a long corridor which was well lit by a row of large windows while providing the necessary security. The parade was to be held at 2.30 p.m. and I was one of the constables on duty that morning, so it was my job to find volunteers. In Ashfordly, it was not easy finding seven youths who looked and dressed like Wayne Waters and in fact, three were located in nearby Brantsford and ferried in by police transport. But by two fifteen, the required seven youthful teddy boys were waiting patiently in an ante-room at the courthouse and being briefed by Detective Sergeant Bedford. Wayne would be brought along by Bedford's assistant and lodged in another ante-room to await his moment of glory.

Sergeant Bedford's assistant that day was a keen young detective who was the force's first member of the newly formed Drugs Squad to be based at Eltering; he had been at that station only a week.

He had been drafted in to assist at the parade because it would give him an opportunity to meet and assess Wayne, ostensibly for future reference. We all felt that Wayne's future would involve drugs, if not now then later. The Drugs Squad officer was Detective Constable Sean O'Kelly, a young Irishman who dressed fashionably and who wore his hair long in keeping with his role as one who must infiltrate the local drugs scene, at that time a fairly new phenomenon in our part of the country. The suspect, Wayne Waters, had been told to dress in the same gear he'd been wearing on the day Ada was attacked – but, of course, he was not quite so foolish and made sure he sported different clothes. He reasoned that if he was not guilty, he should not tempt fate by wearing his famous blue shoes and black leather jacket. He could easily throw the elderly old woman off the scent.

And so it was that eight likely lads formed a straight line along that corridor in the court house. I was guarding the door of the ante-room in which the volunteers had assembled, Sergeant Bedford was in charge and waiting at the door of Wayne's ante-room while DC O'Kelly was standing at the far end of the line-up, a yard or so behind them so as not to be within eye-contact of any of the witnesses. There must be no hint of secret signals being given. Wayne had not brought a friend or a solicitor, his logic being that if he was innocent, why did he need legal representation?

And so, when all the preparations were complete, it was time to bring out Wayne. He emerged with a swagger and a show of confidence and then, having had his rights explained to him, opted to stand at No.6 position.

I think he chose that place because the lads on each side of him were rather similar in looks, age and dress. I'm sure he thought that would help to further baffle Miss Potter. Once he was in the line-up, glancing at his neighbours and making jokes to them, Detective Sergeant Bedford called for silence and asked me to escort Miss Potter from her waiting room. She did not appear in the least nervous at having to endure this procedure and seemed determined to bring to justice the man who had attacked her. I brought her to a halt near Detective Sergeant Bedford who then explained what was expected of her. She must take her time, she could ask the men to undertake small tasks which might help her to make a positive identification and then she must touch the man she had selected. She seemed to understand and began her task.

She started with number one, walking purposefully towards him and looking him up and down very slowly and very carefully before moving along to number two. Then she went back to number one, checked something in her mind, then resumed. And so she went down the line with no signs of nervousness, looking at some of them from the side and one or two from the rear, but there is no doubt she was determined to find her man and equally determined not to be rushed. She would find him, she knew he was here somewhere . . .

And then she reached Wayne Waters who was now standing as stiff as a ramrod and staring over her head, not looking her in the eye and trying not to show any signs of nervousness. I did notice, however, that he was fiddling with the fingers of each hand, opening and closing each fist in a small display of nerves.

And she passed him by. Then she went back for a further look and stared at his face with evident concentration, but again moved on. She looked at the remaining men with a studied calmness, examined each from the side, asked one of them to turn his head to the left just a little, but shook her head. And then, standing a short distance away at the end of the row was Detective Constable O'Kelly.

'That's him, Sergeant, I'd know him anywhere! The one on the end . . .'

And before Detective Sergeant Bedford could point out that she had selected a detective, Wayne let out a cry of celebration.

'Wheyhey!' he yelled, hammering the air with his right fist. 'Wheyhey, she's got him, he's not a bit like me!'

'That's him,' but she now turned to look again at Wayne. 'That shout, I knew it . . . that's what he shouted when he attacked me. Yes, Sergeant, it is not that young man on the end, it is this one,' and without flinching, she strode back, studied Wayne's face with renewed interest, then tapped him on the shoulder. 'I can see him better now . . . yes, there is no doubt. This is the man who stole my handbag.'

'Come along, Wayne,' said Detective Sergeant Bedford. 'I think you've got some explaining to do.'

Wayne was later sentenced to six months' in a Detention Centre.

Chapter 9

Surely the most fascinating part of any police officer's work is the interesting and widely differing range of people we meet in the course of our duty. Apart from routine contact in our towns and villages, whether such people require the services of the constabulary or not, there are those we encounter in their own homes or in holiday accommodation – and homes are always a good indicator of character. With so many of us on the planet, it is not surprising that the variety of personality types is almost endless. There must be many millions of permutations – there are old folks and young ones, serious ones and stupid ones, reliable ones and utterly unreliable ones, criminals and saints, nice people and dreadful ones, persistent complainers and persistent praisers, professionals and amateurs, secretive and open, rich and poor, tall and short, large and small, male and female, black and white . . . as police officers, we meet them all and have to deal with the problems of many, in one way or another. It follows that whenever police officers gather socially, they can be heard telling stories about the fascinating and complex characters they have met in recent times. I am now going to relate some of those tales.

An interesting and rather bizarre story came to light

following the sudden but natural death of a man called Guy Connors. As the village constable, I had to deal with all cases of sudden and unexpected death which occurred on my beat; whenever a doctor declined to certify the cause of death, the case was thoroughly investigated by the police to determine whether or not the death was suspicious in any way. Sudden deaths, usually from natural causes, were a regular feature of our work.

In many cases, a post mortem examination confirmed that death was due to natural causes, so removing any suspicion and the need for a coroner's inquest. In the case of Guy Connors, he had collapsed in one of the fields which surrounded his house on a spectacular hillside site in Rannockdale. His home had earlier been a working farm house, one of the traditional longhouses of our moorlands but Guy, a successful property developer who'd lived locally as a child, had bought the former farm, sold off some of the land and modernized the buildings to transform it into a very fine home.

Such longhouses were built in local stone and comprised two or sometimes three storeys but in days gone by, the cows occupied one end of the building while the farmer and his family lived in the other. In some cases, a very long longhouse might have a small cottage in the middle, this being used by one of the farm labourers' families. If there was not such a cottage within the longhouse, then there may be separate rooms upstairs and downstairs midway along the building, their purpose being to provide accommodation for unmarried farm hands. In examples of the latter case, the house would have two staircases, one for the family and one for the workers – but it was the custom for the workers to take their meals with the family and for the farmer's wife to do their laundry. Such men 'lived-in'. In addition to the labourers' accommodation, there was always the byre, often called the shippen, at the distant end and this was used by the cattle. In the winter months, when the cattle lived permanently indoors, their body heat provided warmth for the entire household. And a few smells!

Guy's house – Stone Ghyll Hall – had been one of those very extensive houses and his alterations meant that the central cottage had become part of his living accommodation. It made a fine and spacious house, with the byre being turned into another cottage. This had not been done with a view to letting it for holidaymakers because he respected his own need for privacy but he told everyone it had been modified to accommodate members of his own family who might like to visit him from time to time. Although he did not have any children, he made it known he had relatives from afar who might want to visit him. In fact, when I arrived in Aidensfield, Guy's cousin lived in that spare cottage – this was typically generous of him because I heard from village gossip that he had offered Gloria the house when she was in desperate need of somewhere to live. She had arrived from Leeds several years before I became the local constable and was still there at the time of this yarn. That act of generosity was typical of him, I was to learn.

Although I was acquainted with Guy, I did not know him very well because I seldom had need to visit his home, either on duty or socially. He kept no livestock and so I did not have to inspect his stock register every quarter although he did own a shotgun and a .22 rifle, consequently I had to renew his shotgun certificate and firearm certificate when they were due. Guy was in his mid fifties, a sturdy red haired man with an infectious laugh and a rather portly figure. He always smartly dressed in countryman's clothing – tweed jackets, cavalry twill trousers and brogue shoes or perhaps stout leather boots, and he seemed to love the way of life in rural Yorkshire.

He drove a Land Rover and a blue Jaguar, while his wife, Sue, had a neat little red MG sports car. Sue did not have a job of any kind but found plenty to occupy her in and around Rannockdale. She was, in fact, a very talented landscape artist and some of her watercolours were regularly on display in local galleries.

Guy's offices were in York but he worked from home whenever he could and so he was often to be seen in and around Rannockdale, and frequently in Ashfordly where he went to see people like his bank manager and solicitors. Everyone liked Guy – that was the reaction I got whenever I mentioned his name – and no one had a bad word for Sue either. They were a lovely couple who were regarded as 'locals'.

Guy had made a lot of money but had not been spoilt by his success; he would chat cheerfully to anyone in the pub where he would pop in for a pint some evenings and was very generous with both his money and his time so far as local events and charities were concerned. Whenever a church fête or other fund-raising event was held in the village, Guy could be relied upon not only to make a handsome donation but also to help in a more practical way, either by running a stall, being the master of ceremonies or even acting as an unpaid taxi-driver for people without their own transport. On occasions, he had even offered his fields for events – a village gymkhana was held in his grounds on one occasion and on another he had allowed his fields to be used for a village sports day. Nothing was too much trouble for him, no voluntary job too humble for him to take. His wife and his charming cousin were equally generous with their time and could be relied upon to help, often working side by side on stalls or helping with the tea at a village cricket match.

In short, the people of Rannockdale felt very proud to have such a fine fellow living among them, a local lad who had done well.

It was a huge shock for everyone when he died so suddenly. He had been walking his two golden retrievers at the time, a task he undertook every morning before breakfast and when he did not return at his usual time, Sue Connors thought he must have found someone to chat to, or had perhaps taken a longer route. When another hour went by with no word from him, she decided to make a search. She knew the route he always took and set off – it was a fine, dry morning in early March with just the hint of a frost in the air. She found him lying in a field with his two faithful dogs at his side, both whining.

For a few minutes she did not know what to do because she had no idea whether or not he was dead but after futile attempts to revive him, she ran all the way back to the house with the dogs trotting behind and rang for the doctor and an ambulance. Then she went to inform cousin Gloria who was having breakfast in her cottage. Gloria said she would rush out to remain with him while Susan waited for the doctor; he, and the ambulance driver, would have to be shown to the scene. Doctor William Williams, the fiery Welsh doctor from Ashfordly, had not then started his surgery in town and so he rushed out to Rannockdale, a drive of about twenty minutes. The ambulance, responding to Susan's 999 call, was also en route within minutes but when Doctor Williams certified that Guy was dead, the ambulance had to return to its station. It could not be used to carry bodies which were already dead; the purpose of an ambulance was to transport the living.

Although Dr Williams could certify the fact that Guy was dead, he could not certify the cause of death and so he had to call the police who would treat this as a sudden and unexplained death with the inevitable investigation. It meant the body must remain where it was until the police had attended and examined the scene. And that is how I became involved.

'PC Rhea, Aidensfield,' I answered my phone that morning.

'Dr Williams here, ringing from Stone Ghyll Hall, Rannockdale, constable. I'm afraid I have some bad news, a sudden death. Guy Connors, he's lying in one of his fields. There are no injuries and no reason to think this is suspicious in any way. It seems he collapsed and died on the spot while walking his dogs this morning but as I've not treated him in recent months, I cannot certify the cause of his death. It'll mean a postmortem, PC Rhea, you know the routine.' And he gave me directions to help me reach the body.

'I'll be right there,' I said.

Before leaving, I rang Ashfordly Police Station to tell the office duty constable where I was heading and why; Alf Ventress answered.

'Oh dear,' he said. 'He will be missed, Guy was such a decent chap, most affable. You'll need the box, will you?'

'And a helping hand to lift it,' I added.

'I'll bring it myself,' Alf assured me, and so I told him where to find the body. The box was a make-shift coffin complete with a lid, all made of strong brown plastic, and it was used by the police to transport bodies to a mortuary.

It was frequently used at the scenes of sudden death like this one, or perhaps following a traffic accident or suicide. Guy's body would have to be taken to Ashfordly General Hospital for the necessary post mortem, and that task would require the box. It served to conceal the body from public view and to transport it with some decorum.

'I'll leave a note for the sergeant to tell him where we've gone,' said Alf. 'He's out at the moment, doing some early turn visits. There's no reason to think this is a suspicious death, is there? I mean, do I need to notify CID?'

'Dr Williams thinks Guy collapsed and died on the spot,' I said. 'He said there are no injuries and has no reason to think this is a suspicious death. He's called us because he can't certify the cause of death, he's not treated Guy for a long time.'

'Fair enough, it sounds pretty routine to me. All right, Nick, you get yourself out there to do what you can and I'll follow very soon.'

Most constables in rural police forces were accustomed to dealing with sudden deaths of this kind; in the larger boroughs and cities, however, this duty was performed by one constable who was appointed the full-time Coroner's Officer. His entire duty involved dealing with sudden and unexplained deaths which meant that other constables in town did not gain the wider and more valuable experience enjoyed by their rural counterparts. Because I was now charged with the duty of dealing with this death, I became the Coroner's Office for that particular case; it was my task to investigate all the circumstances, to organize and attend the postmortem, to submit a report and to liaise with the coroner.

If the postmortem examination showed death was due to natural causes, perhaps a heart attack, then there would probably be no inquest. Whether or not there was to be an inquest was a matter for the coroner, his decision being based on the police report.

Dealing with unexpected deaths of this kind was never easy because we had to do our duty and establish the truth by asking a lot of searching and at times very personal questions but at the same time we had to bear in mind the sorrow of the family who had so tragically lost a dear one. Nevertheless, all such cases were full of interest – they were rather like a modified version of a murder enquiry.

When I arrived at Stone Ghyll Hall, I went to the kitchen door. Susan was inside, sitting at a table and drinking a coffee with Guy's cousin, Gloria. I introduced myself and said I would go alone to examine Guy if they could direct me to where he was lying, adding that a colleague would soon be arriving with a vehicle. Susan, tearful but in control, asked if I wanted a coffee but I declined at this stage, saying, 'Perhaps later, thank you, I'll need to talk to you once I have examined the scene.' I did not say aloud, 'and your husband's body.'

As I approached, I could see the body lying crumpled in the field. It was not covered and there was no one in attendance for this was a remote place, well out of sight of any house or road and so I stood close to the corpse, first examining it from a short distance before making a sketch of its position in relation to key points, like the field gate, a telephone pole and a mound of rock protruding from the grass. Next, I approached Guy to look for any signs of physical injury.

He was lying in a prone position on his left side, almost

as if he had curled up and gone to sleep and I could not see any injuries or blood, neither was his clothing torn or dirty. Then I had to turn him over to gain a closer look at his left features, for they were hidden beneath his body, but there was nothing. I did all the usual tests and observations – no weapon at the scene, no blood oozing from ears, mouth, nose and no cuts or bruises, no sign of broken limbs, no torn clothing, no sign of interference with him, no torn clothing in his fists, no dog bites, all clothing intact with shoes on his feet . . . I felt this kind of initial examination placed a huge burden on a constable but that is how things were done in the 1960s – and, of course, I had the benefit of having had the body examined earlier by a professional and highly experienced doctor.

Having examined the scene and the body, and completed my sketch complete with corpse, I was undecided whether to return to the house to begin my enquiries, or to await Alf Ventress here. And then I saw him heading towards me. He was driving the large dark blue police estate car which was based at Sub-Divisional Headquarters in Eltering, and in the rear I could see the box. The vehicle bounced and groaned across the uneven surface of the field and came to a rest at my side. Alf clambered out, came to look at Guy's body and after closely inspecting it for a minute or two, said, 'Heart attack, Nick, mark my words. You've finished here, have you?'

'Not quite, I've still got to interview the widow and the deceased's cousin,' I said.

'Right, well, let's get him loaded up and I'll take him to Ashfordly morgue. I'll get help lifting him out when I get there, you stay here to get finished whatever you have to do. I'll have words with them at the morgue and hopefully, they'll be able to give me a time for the PM.'

And so it was that as Guy's mortal remains were removed, I returned to the kitchen where Sue Connors invited me in for a coffee. Now, I really felt as if I needed one. Cousin Gloria had now left and I guessed Sue would welcome the opportunity to occupy herself, even by doing something simple like making me a coffee. A very handsome woman in her late forties, she was well spoken, articulate and highly attractive with large brown eyes and a head of beautifully kept hair. Now she looked very pale and her eyes were red from weeping but she insisted she was able to talk to me and knew I had to ask her a lot of questions. This kind of interview was never easy but it helped having a mug of coffee at my elbow, and it also helped having such a calm person as this so recently-bereaved lady. My job was to establish the last known movements of Guy Connors, starting with yesterday evening, listing what he had eaten and drunk since then, what he had done with his time, whether they'd had a row or fight of any kind, large or small, whether anyone else could corroborate her statement, whether he was heavily insured, what his financial circumstances were really like and whether anyone was known to be antagonistic towards Guy. Fatalistic anger was not unknown in the harsh world of some businesses; professional jealousy or untrustworthiness could result in all manner of vicious retaliation.

Sue chattered amiably about other things whilst answering my questions and I responded to her side remarks, for they provided constant but momentarily welcome diversions from my not-too-subtle interrogation. She told me a little about Guy's family. His parents were dead but he had a brother in New Zealand and an uncle still living in

Canada, both of whom she had yet to inform about his death. Guy's other uncles and aunts had died some years ago but she told me he had lots of cousins all over the world, although she did not know any of them, except Gloria. Those living overseas rarely got in touch, not even with Christmas cards, but Gloria had promised to contact anyone with whom she was still in touch. Even though he had been born in Rannockdale, Guy's links with the village had ended during his childhood, yet he still regarded this place as home.

What emerged from my enquiries was that the Connors appeared to be a loving couple with a busy life but who liked to be with one another when Guy was not at work. They had spent yesterday evening together without any kind of dispute or anger; after a meal of steak followed by a fruit salad they'd watched television for a while and had then enjoyed a walk along the lane outside their home before going to bed. Susan had gone up to bed while Guy had locked the house and put the dogs to bed in their outbuilding, then this morning he had got up at his usual time of 7 a.m. and called upstairs to say he was taking the retrievers out for their morning walk, as he always did. When he'd gone, she got up and sat down to her breakfast while awaiting his return . . . but today he'd not come back.

I wrote down her words in the form of a long statement which she signed as being true to the best of her knowledge, and then I explained about the postmortem, following with advice about the procedures involving the death certificate and burial in such cases. I told her I did not think an inquest would be necessary which in turn meant there should be no hold-up in the funeral arrangements. I assured her I would keep in touch and would relay to her the result of the postmortem once it was known. I then told her I must interview Gloria to see whether she had seen Guy in those last minutes before his death. She and Gloria appeared to be the only witnesses to his life in those final fifteen hours or so. Sue told me that Guy would often pop in for a chat with Gloria because she was so alone but she doubted whether he would have done so this morning before his daily walk with the dogs.

When I knocked on Gloria's door, she answered almost immediately, clearly having been awaiting my arrival and I could see she had been crying. She was now trying to compose herself and from her demeanour I gained an immediate impression that she was worried about something. Her future in this house perhaps? I wondered whether she had a job of any kind, or some sort of profession to follow. Perhaps she should have been at work this morning?

'Come in,' she led me into a very pleasant lounge and indicated an easy chair, asking if I'd like a coffee. I declined, having just enjoyed one with Susan, then explained my need to talk to her about Guy's last known movements. She indicated her understanding and I began my interrogation by asking for her full name.

'Gloria Jean Firth,' she smiled sadly, and I recorded her address as Stone Ghyll Cottage, Rannockdale.

'And you are Guy's cousin?' I began.

At this apparently innocuous question, she hesitated, then asked, 'These enquiries, the ones you are making, it's all part of the legal process, isn't it? Courts and things, the inquest and all that.'

'Yes, even if there is no inquest into Guy's death, this is still a very formal investigation. The statements I take from witnesses like yourself are all official documents.'

'Oh dear,' it was clear that something was seriously bothering her. 'Guy would never have expected this, never . . . PC Rhea, I must be honest with you, really I must but I must also ask for discretion.'

'Well, I'll be as discreet as I can,' I was wondering whether she was not wanting her age to be recorded anywhere. Some ladies were very touchy about that. 'I can tell you that these statements will not become public unless there is an inquest and I doubt if there will be one in this instance. Like Dr Williams, I am sure Guy's death is not in the least suspicious. I am sure the post mortem will confirm the doctor's opinion that he died from natural causes.'

'I am not Guy's cousin,' she blurted out before I could continue. 'Please do not enter that I am his cousin, I'm not. I must tell the truth.'

'Oh,' I was not quite expecting this, and, to be honest, did not think it really mattered who she was.

She was living alone in a cottage attached to Guy's home, just as anyone else might have been. From my point of view, she was merely a potential witness but before I could say it didn't really matter who she was, she blurted out another surprise.

'I'm his mistress, I have been for years, he gives me an allowance . . . Sue does not know this but it will all come out now . . . oh, God, this is dreadful. What am I going to do? She'll kick me out of here when she finds out . . .'

I was not sure how to react to this revelation. 'You mean his wife has no idea of your relationship? Even though you live in the same building?'

'That's right, I've always been his mistress, for more than

twenty years, twenty five or whatever. A long time. To get me here, he told her I was a cousin in need of accommodation and she has made me most welcome, over all these years, even when he's been popping in here to be with me . . . you'd think she must have guessed but she hasn't . . . and she's such a nice woman . . .' Then she burst into a flood of tears.

'Look,' I said when she had calmed down a little. 'You realize this could make all the difference to my enquiries. Think of it like this – suppose Susan had discovered the relationship, might she have done something to Guy by way of revenge?' I was thinking of how wronged women would sometimes resort to poison as an act of revenge or worse, but I added, 'If Susan genuinely has no idea, then of course she would not want to take revenge on her husband.'

'I knew it would all come out, I told Guy it couldn't work, me living so close to him and Susan. . . .'

'Look,' I said. 'All I want from you at this stage is a simple statement telling me what you know about the way Guy spent his final hours. I don't think your personal relationship with him is material at this stage, that's pending the outcome of the postmortem of course. If that determines Guy's death was from natural causes, it will eliminate all suspicion of foul play and, in my opinion, that makes your relationship irrelevant. If the postmortem does reveal something untoward, however, then I shall have to make your relationship known. As things are, therefore, my initial enquiries will show that you are a lady who is living in a cottage adjoining Stone Ghyll Hall, someone who knows Guy Connors and can help in describing his final hours. It's nothing more than that. But, I repeat, if the postmortem does show anything sinister, then I am duty bound to take this further. That is the gamble you have to take. I am not covering up for you, Miss Firth, I am merely adopting a sensible approach to what might became a difficult personal situation for you when all this is over.'

'I'm prepared for that but what about my home? Sue is bound to suspect the worse, she'll surely want me to leave.'

'That's not a matter for me or any police officer,' I said. 'It will depend on Susan's decision about her future. My enquiries are not to make moral judgements, just to establish what caused Guy to die so suddenly.'

'We are good friends, we really are, Sue and I . . .' she was saying as the tears cascaded down her cheeks.

I recorded in her statement that Guy had popped in to see her before taking the dogs out that morning, but it was merely for a chat and nothing more. At the time, he'd appeared his usual cheerful self with no signs of illness, and he was talking about driving over to York and taking Sue with him later in the day. Gloria could not add anything else which would materially help my enquiries.

Later that day, the postmortem proved Guy had suffered a massive heart attack. Beyond any doubt, death was from natural causes and the coroner decided against an inquest. I did not have to reveal what I knew about Gloria's relationship with Guy. Whether or not Susan Connors ever knew about the true relationship will never be known, but Gloria remained in the cottage and Susan continued to live at the Hall. They went everywhere together and were clearly the best of friends.

I have often wondered whether I did the right thing by keeping Gloria's secret but it did occur to me later that if Guy had been injured in some way, however slightly, or there had been any suggestion of poison in his body, this could have developed into a murder investigation with two prime suspects.

Whether Susan Connors was a very foolish woman or a very clever one is something which can be debated for a long, long time, but not long after I had dealt with her husband's death, I encountered another instance of curious human behaviour in Rannockdale. Like the Connors story, it contained strong elements of secrecy but this time by a greater number of people because it involved all those who lived in that small community deep in the North York Moors.

Rannockdale is a broad valley deep within the heart of the North York Moors National Park and much of it comprises remote farmsteads and lonely cottages high in the dale. Known for the bluebells which flourish along the banks of the beck which flows down from the moors, there is a village which bears the same name as the dale, i.e. Rannockdale. It is a tightly-knit community of fewer than sixty moorfolk who live in a cluster of cottages at the foot of the dale. These are small stone-built homes of considerable age and they are tightly packed in a hollow beside the beck, as if sheltering from the chill winds and ferocious weather which can sometimes assail this area. During my time as the local constable, there was a tiny shop in the front room of one of the houses; a disused Methodist chapel had been converted into another home while yet another larger cottage was also the Rannockdale Arms. It had just one tiny bar which was tended by the lady of the house, Mrs Trinder, whose husband worked on a nearby farm. The pub was open only during weekday evenings and on Saturdays, but was closed every Sunday. It held one of the few six-day liquor licences in the district.

The Rannockdale Arms was really a rather small bed-and-breakfast establishment which happened to have a licence to sell wines, beers and spirits. Its licensee, Mrs Trinder, earned a modest income from her bed-and-breakfast business, aided by the availability of alcoholic drinks. Because it was officially classified as licensed premises, I had to pay regular visits as part of my duty, just to ensure the licensing laws were not being broken or abused.

Mrs Trinder always seemed to have visitors staying in her modest establishment, even out of season and this might have been because it was far from the madding crowds; there is no doubt it was a comfortable place and her food was renowned in the district but one of the chief attractions was the wealth of interesting walks, historical associations and other fascinating villages in the locality. There was always plenty of things for tourists and visitors to see and do, and the coast was only an hour's drive away. One example of the ever-lasting popularity of the Rannockdale Arms was revealed by a couple who came back every year, always wanting the same bedroom, the same food and even going to the same places they had previously visited. They were George and Ethel Barlow from Hemel Hempstead.

When I first met them, they would be in their mid-sixties, a small and quiet couple who drove a tiny grey Austin A35. Both wore grey clothing and had rimless spectacles; they almost looked anonymous in a crowd and both were now retired from their jobs as clerical officers in a local council office. I was patrolling Rannockdale and had parked my minivan near the shop to enable me to spend a few minutes on foot in the centre of this tiny place.

It was around ten fifteen one Tuesday morning in May and I noticed the Barlows emerge from the Rannockdale

Arms. They saw me and waved, calling 'Good morning, officer.'

'Good morning,' I returned. 'A nice day.'

'You might be able to help us,' the man came closer. 'We're thinking of having a day on the coast and wondered if you could suggest a nice place to go. We don't want to go to Whitby or Scarborough, they get too busy with tourists and we've been there quite a lot anyway. We'd prefer somewhere with a nice open beach and no amusement arcades or noisy people.'

'Try Sandsend,' I suggested. 'It's further along the coast from Whitby, or you could even try Runswick Bay or Staithes – or even Skinningrove's hidden little gem of a beach, away from the rather grotty main area. And to the south of Whitby there's always Robin Hood's Bay or Ravenscar.'

We discussed the merits of these places and how to get there, and then he told me his name was George Barlow from Hemel Hempstead, and that he and his wife, Ethel, had been coming to Rannockdale every spring without a break for the last twenty years. In fact, they had also come here for about ten years before World War II but George's war-time service had interrupted their routine. Now, they were continuing their visits and with pride, he told me they always used the same room at the inn, they ate the same meals as they had always done, and usually visited the same places. On this occasion, though, they were feeling adventurous, hence the request for advice on some other charming coastal places.

'We've always been made so very welcome here,' George added. 'We join the locals in the bar of an evening and sometimes they have a sing-song which we join, we know everyone by their first names, we've been asked to visit them in their homes and of course, we know Madge in the shop, she can get whatever we want for picnics and so on. It's really wonderful, constable, you are so lucky to live and work in such a delightful place among such lovely people.'

It was evident the Barlows thought they had found their heaven on earth and I watched as they boarded their little car and set off to explore the magnificent North Riding coastline. As I pottered somewhat aimlessly around the village for a few minutes, I noticed a van ease to a halt a few hundred yards along the lane, and then a man shouted and waved to catch my attention. This was indeed a busy morning for Rannockdale!

'Yes?' I called back as I approached him.

'I'm looking for Heather Cottage,' he said.

'Behind me,' I knew where it was. 'Straight on past the shop for about half a mile, it's on the roadside, on the left. A pretty place built of local stone, it's got a small garden in front of it, with a green gate. The name's on the gate, you can't miss it.'

'It's empty and is up for sale, the Rannockdale Estate's decided to get rid of it,' he said. 'I've got to place a "For Sale" sign in the garden. Thanks.'

With no more excitements in the village, I returned to my van and headed down the dale towards Brantsford where I was due to make another foot patrol for about an hour. This would be a busier time, but I knew the Rannockdale villagers would have been pleased to note the presence of a uniformed bobby among them, if only for a short time once in a while.

I thought no more of my chat with the Barlows until about three weeks later when I was again in Brantsford, this time on market day, a Wednesday. As I was moving among the crowds of people and traffic, I was suddenly aware of Mr Barlow heading towards me. He was alone. He saw and recognized me at the same instant I recognized him and halted with a large and happy smile on his face.

'Ah, Constable, we met in Rannockdale, didn't we? A few weeks ago.'

'Yes,' I said. 'You were on holiday and heading for the coast.'

'Thank you for your suggestions, yes. We found Sandsend, a lovely place, and went to Staithes and Runswick Bay as you suggested. We're saving Robin Hood's Bay and Ravenscar for another time . . . but guess what! Our dream has come true! We can't really believe our good luck, but it's happened. Our life-time dream is about to be fulfilled.'

'Dream?' I remembered him saying how he and his wife had come on holiday to the Rannockdale Arms year after year, and how much they adored the locality.

'We've been in love with Rannockdale for years and years,' he said. 'We could never think of living here because of our work, so we had to be content with holidays. That's why we came so often, every holiday in fact. We're in love with the place, I think. Anyway, would you believe it! We're both retired now and have no ties in Hemel Hempstead, then when we were here last time, we saw a cottage for sale. Heather Cottage. I mean, what a coincidence . . . it's almost as if it was meant for us.'

'I saw the man heading there with the sale notice,' I smiled.

'We spotted it that very day, on our way back from Staithes. If we hadn't come that way back from the coast, we might have missed it. Talk about a piece of good luck! The timing is just right, it couldn't be more perfect. And the house is ideal for us, not too large and not too small, although it needs some attention. But we've bought it. We're selling our bungalow in Hemel Hempstead and have bought Heather Cottage. We expect to move in sometime during August. I'm just going to see the estate agent now to settle a few details.'

'Congratulations!' I could see he was brimming over with delight and happiness at the prospect of seeing his long-term dream fulfilled and was genuinely pleased for him. 'I'm really pleased for you.'

'You must call and see us when we are settled in,' he invited. 'Maybe I could persuade you to have a celebratory sherry with us! Or a coffee at least!'

'I'll remember to call, my name is PC Rhea,' I told him and off he went, almost overcome by his boundless excitement and expectations of sheer happiness.

In the weeks that followed, Mr and Mrs Barlow moved into Heather Cottage to continue their love affair with Rannockdale and it was in late September when I was next in the village with time to spare. On this occasion, I had a purpose – a local resident's firearms certificate was due for renewal and I had arranged to meet him. When I had dealt with that matter I had about an hour before my next commitment and recalled Mr and Mrs Barlow's invitation to pop in for a coffee. I decided to walk the short distance, if only to display the uniform.

But when I approached Heather Cottage, I saw a 'For Sale' sign in the garden. It bore the same Estate Agent's name as on that earlier occasion. As I opened the garden gate and strode up the path towards the house, I could see into the lounge. It was full of packing cases and there was more evidence of furniture and crockery being stacked ready for removal. I wondered if I had misunderstood the Barlows – perhaps they were just moving in? Or had moved in very recently? But from his lounge, George spotted me in his garden and opened the window to call me.

'Come round to the kitchen door, Mr Rhea,' he called. 'It's the only place we can sit down. Ethel is about to make some coffee, so you'll join us?'

Moments later, I was sitting at their tiny kitchen table as Ethel busied herself with the coffee, and so I said, 'Look, I won't stay long, I'm in the way. I didn't realize you were just settling in.'

'Settling in? No, Mr Rhea, we're not, we're moving out. We're going back to Hemel Hempstead.'

'Going back?' I was both surprised and shocked. 'But I thought this was where you always wanted to be. . . .'

'It was,' snapped George. 'We loved the place, we loved the area and the people, we'd done so for years and years and thought we'd like to settle here, to live here for ever. But it hasn't worked out.'

'Can I ask why?'

'I don't know,' he shrugged his thin shoulders. 'The minute we got unpacked, Ethel and I went down to the Rannockdale Arms to say hello to everyone, like we used to do when we arrived on holiday, but no one would speak to us.'

'Why not?'

'We don't know, Mr Rhea, we just don't know. For some reason they liked us coming here on holiday, but don't like us living here. Nobody's given any reason, there's been no angry words or fighting, it's just clear they don't want us living among them. They don't speak to us in the pub or in the shop, and pass us by on the other side of the street. And we've done nothing, except move into Heather Cottage.'

'I can't believe this!' I cried. 'They're always so nice and friendly.'

'They were, always nice and friendly, lovely people. Friends, so we thought. But now they don't want to know us, so we're returning to Hemel Hempstead.'

'I'm sorry,' I said. 'Truly, I am, and I can't offer any reason either, no one's said anything to me about this.'

And so I had a coffee with them, wished them better luck in their return to the south and continued my patrol. No one in Rannockdale mentioned this odd behaviour to me either and, knowing how country folk could sometimes behave, I did not believe there had been a concerted or organized effort to oust the newcomers, nor were the Barlows disliked. Their misery could have resulted from individuals taking it upon themselves not to speak to them and also not allowing themselves to be seen actively encouraging the permanent residency of the Barlows. Clearly, the locals did not like strangers joining their community on a permanent basis.

It seemed to me that that kind of individual tendency was akin to group activity, rather like birds and animals rejecting one who is different, such as an albino. If one local person saw fit to reject the Barlows, the others would do likewise. If I had asked any of the locals why the Barlows were not welcome, I doubt if I would have received a knowledgeable answer – probably because, in truth, there was no real answer. I don't think anyone had openly rejected them and the only comment I heard came a few weeks later when I was in the bar of the tiny inn and overheard someone say,

'Well, them Barlows weren't really t'right sort o' folks for a small spot like this.'

I think the experiences and expectations of holiday makers and visitors are quite different from people actually living in a small community, especially those who have lived there as natives and I wondered how the Barlows might be treated if they returned for another holiday? I would guess they would be treated just as they had been prior to their decision to live in Rannockdale. Visitors were not the same as locals! Having said that, I doubted they would ever return for another holiday.

Perhaps it is true what they say in Yorkshire – that there's nowt so queer as folk.

The third tale also involved very strong elements of secrecy – and a marvellous example of hidden generosity. It began when the recently widowed Mrs Amy Price hailed me as I was patrolling Aidensfield's main street. In her early seventies, she was a small woman with a pinched elfin type of face and a mop of pure white hair.

She was washing the windows at the front of her cottage and noticed me as I was walking past.

'Mr Rhea,' she called, dropping the leather into her bucket. 'Can you spare me a minute?'

'Yes, of course.'

'Come in then, I'll put the kettle on.'

This kind of hospitality was a feature of village life in rural Yorkshire and so, within moments, I was sitting before her fireside with a cup of tea and a large slice of fruit cake, still wondering why she wanted to speak to me.

'You'll be wondering what this is all about, Mr Rhea,' she smiled cheerfully. 'Well, it's not to complain, I can tell you that, but I have received this.'

She reached up to the mantelpiece and lifted down a white envelope of the kind that might have contained a birthday or Christmas card. She handed it to me. It was quite bulky due to its thick contents but bore no name or address, and it had been opened. I wondered what I was supposed to do with it.

'Go on, look inside,' she ordered.

I obeyed and found it full of money, all in pound notes.

'There's fifty,' she said. 'Fifty pounds, and nothing to say where it's come from.'

'Did you find it in the street?' My first thought was that she wished to report this to me as an item of found property.

'No,' she smiled. 'It came through my letter box a few days ago. It was there on the mat when I got up, it must have come very early or very late the night before because I never heard the letter box clatter.'

'So who sent it?'

'I don't know,' she shrugged her thin shoulders. 'That's the problem you see. I have no idea where it's come from. I am worried that it might not be for me, you see, that somebody might have pushed it through the wrong letter box.'

'If they had made a mistake, I'd have thought they would have realized by now and come back to retrieve it.'

'That's what I thought as well, Mr Rhea, which is why I am keeping it on my mantelpiece, just in case.'

'Do you think it might be money owed to your husband?' Frank Price had been a self-employed electrician and I wondered if this was payment for some job he'd undertaken before his death.

'No, Frank kept very good records, Mr Rhea, and everyone has paid him. Anyhow, I thought you'd better know about this, in case somebody comes asking for it. I don't want people to think I might have kept it when it doesn't belong to me. I have asked my neighbours on both sides if it might be theirs, and it's not, so I just don't know where it's come from. I thought it best to report it to you.'

'I'll treat it as found property,' I told her. 'That means it will be entered in our records and if anyone does report losing it, we can restore it to them.'

'That's what I would like,' she smiled.

I continued, 'I suppose it's possible someone lost it in the street outside your house and someone else thought it might belong to you, so they pushed it through your letter box. That's just a passing thought ... but it might not be like that at all! Anyway, Mrs Price, the situation is that you must keep it for three months, and if it's not claimed in that time, you can regard it as yours.'

'You don't take it away then?'

'No, we prefer finders of money to keep it, Mrs Price, it saves space in our offices and avoids a lot of unnecessary paperwork. If someone does report losing it, we will contact you.'

'I will not spend a penny of it, Mr Rhea.'

'You can after three months, Mrs Price, if it's not claimed.'

We chatted for a further twenty minutes or so as I enjoyed her cake and tea, with Amy telling me about how she'd coped since her husband's death. A popular man around Aidensfield and district, he'd been nearly seventy-seven when he'd died but had kept working, albeit with fewer hours, because his savings and modest pension had not been sufficient to maintain his former lifestyle. He'd been happy to keep working so that he earned bits of cash for 'extras', as he called it. Now, she admitted, her income had been drastically reduced but, as she said, 'I can get by, Mr Rhea, I have no debts and we've always saved for a rainy day, the house is paid for so I can cope even if it is difficult replacing my old fridge or washing machine. I do need a new washing machine so I'm saving hard. It's that sort of big expenditure I find hard now Frank's gone.'

I gathered from those final comments that she was finding life something of a struggle. The mystery of Ada's windfall puzzled me for a while but I soon forgot about it as I went about my other duties, and then I was heading for the post office when I overheard two young mothers chatting outside. One of them said, 'But I have no idea who sent it, June. It just came through the letter box, twenty-five pounds in a white envelope. No name, nothing.'

The young mum called June noticed my arrival and stopped me. 'Just tell Mr Rhea about this, Sandra, he might know something about it, or what you should do.'

And so I learned of another mystery gift of money. Sandra did volunteer the information that her husband, John, had been out of work for three weeks due to a broken ankle, and it was a case of 'no work, no pay.' With a small child to care for, life was never easy and then out of the blue, a white envelope containing £25 in notes had arrived through the letter box with no indication who had sent it. I treated this in the same way I'd dealt with Amy Price – it was recorded as found property and she would hang on to the money for three months, then it would be regarded as hers if it was not claimed.

When the third similar instance came to my notice, I realized that Aidensfield was being targetted by a generous but secretive benefactor. The third beneficiary was the Anglican parish church. A hole had developed in the roof and it was letting in water; the problem had been temporarily solved by placing a large bucket in the aisle beneath the gap but an inspection of the roof had revealed some rotten timbers and much more of a problem than a mere loose tile or a hole.

A considerable amount of restorative work was urgently needed with the cost expected to be upwards of £1000, something a small parish like Aidensfield could barely afford without some kind of external help. And then £1000 in notes had arrived at the vicarage in a white envelope with no indication of the sender's name or address. The vicar did his best, through posters in the shop, post office and church noticeboard, to persuade the secretive donor to reveal his or her identity so that adequate appreciation could be expressed, but there was nothing. No one admitted sending the money – but the roof was repaired without any further debt being incurred.

Over the weeks and months which followed, I became aware of no less than eight other instances of similar anonymous generosity. In every case the money had been placed in a plain white envelope of the kind which was on sale at any stationery shop, and there was never any indication of the donor's name or address. What did emerge was that all the benefactors were genuinely in need of financial aid, usually of a temporary nature. One was the wife of a man who spent all his money on drink instead of giving some to her to clothe and feed their three children; another was an elderly man who'd been faced with an unexpectedly heavy electricity bill after a cold winter and another was a middle-aged woman who'd had her handbag snatched moments after placing £500 into it, money she'd just drawn from the bank in Ashfordly to pay for her uninsured mother's funeral.

All the cases were deserving and it was inevitable that these acts would generate gossip in the village.

People began to wonder who was going to be the next to benefit in this way but it was clear that the donor was very selective – as time went by, it was clear that people who wasted money were not likely to receive such a windfall. Spendthifts and wastrels, or those who deliberately tried to win the attention of the donor, were not likely to benefit. It was only those who, for reasons not of their own making, had fallen on hard times but the chief cause of speculation was the identity of the mystery benefactor.

Was it someone living in Aidensfield? Or someone living nearby, perhaps doing the same thing in other villages? What was known was that the money always arrived either late at night or very early in the morning, always in a white envelope and always anonymously.

Who, in this remote rural area, had sufficient money to be so generous, giving away cash in amounts ranging from £25 up to £1000 without wanting any kind of thanks? I thought I knew everyone living in Aidensfield well enough to identify someone who might be so very generous, but I could not produce any likely names. I wondered if it was someone living away from the village, perhaps passing through during the hours of darkness, probably on foot, to deliver those white envelopes. In many ways, it was very like the work of the original Father Christmas!

From my point of view, the biggest mystery was how the benefactor became aware of the very personal circumstances of the recipients. How could he or she possibly identify genuine people in need without those people becoming aware of such a close interest in their affairs?

Apart from the gift to the church, was there a common factor which linked all the other recipients? A relative of all perhaps? A former employer? A friend of a friend? Someone who was regularly in Aidensfield like a businessman or some wealthy person with a social conscience? Or could it be one of our Aidensfield residents with a close interest in, and deep knowledge of, our village people?

To my knowledge, the gifts continued for about three and a half years, always to deserving recipients, but I never heard of similar events in any of the nearby communities like Elsinby, Briggsby or Crampton although I am sure further gifts were given to people in Aidensfield without my knowledge.

And there the mystery remains. It is one of those few rural secrets that have remained a secret throughout the passing of the years.